LOVE IS ENOUGH

OR

THE FREEING OF PHARAMOND

A MORALITY.

BY

WILLIAM MORRIS

THIRD EDITION.

LONDON:

REEVES AND TURNER, 196, STRAND.

1889.

William Morris (24 March 1834 – 3 October 1896) was an English textile designer, poet, novelist, translator, and socialist activist. Associated with the British Arts and Crafts Movement, he was a major contributor to the revival of traditional British textile arts and methods of production. His literary contributions helped to establish the modern fantasy genre, while he played a significant role in propagating the early socialist movement in Britain.

Born in Walthamstow, Essex, to a wealthy middle-class family, Morris came under the strong influence of medievalism while studying Classics at Oxford University, there joining the Birmingham Set. After university, he trained as an architect, married Jane Burden, and developed close friendships with the Pre-Raphaelite artists Edward Burne-Jones and Dante Gabriel Rossetti and with the Neo-Gothic architect Philip Webb. Webb and Morris designed a family home, Red House, then in Kent, where the latter lived from 1859 to 1865, before moving to Bloomsbury, central London. In 1861, Morris founded a decorative arts firm with Burne-Jones, Rossetti, Webb, and others: the Morris, Marshall, Faulkner & Co. Becoming highly fashionable and much in demand, the firm profoundly influenced interior decoration throughout the Victorian period, with Morris designing tapestries, wallpaper, fabrics, furniture, and stained glass windows. In 1875, Morris assumed total control of the company, which was renamed Morris & Co.

Although retaining a main home in London, from 1871 Morris rented the rural retreat of Kelmscott Manor, Oxfordshire. Greatly influenced by visits to Iceland, with Eiríkr Magnússon he produced a series of English-language translations of Icelandic Sagas. He also achieved success with the publication of his epic poems and novels, namely The Earthly Paradise (1868–1870), A Dream of John Ball (1888), the utopian News from Nowhere (1890), and the fantasy romance The Well at the World's End (1896). In 1877 he founded the Society for the Protection of Ancient Buildings to campaign against the damage caused by architectural restoration. Embracing Marxism and influenced by anarchism, in the 1880s Morris became a committed revolutionary socialist activist; after an involvement in the Social Democratic Federation (SDF), he founded the Socialist League in 1884, but broke with that organization in 1890. In 1891 he founded the Kelmscott Press to publish limited-edition, illuminated-style print books, a cause to which he devoted his final years.

Morris is recognised as one of the most significant cultural figures of Victorian Britain; though best known in his lifetime as a poet, he posthumously became better known for his designs. Founded in 1955, the William Morris Society is devoted to his legacy, while multiple biographies and studies of his work have seen publication. Many of the buildings associated with his life are open to visitors, much of his work can be found in art galleries and museums, and his designs are still in production.

DRAMATIS PERSONS
  GILES,
  Peasant-folk. JOAN, his Wife,
  THE EMPEROR. THE EMPRESS. THE MAYOR.
  A COUNCILLOR.
  MASTER OLIVER, King Pharamond's Foster- father.
  A NORTHERN LORD.
  KING PHARAMOND.
  AZALAIS, his Love.
  KING THEOBALD.
  HONORIUS, the Councillor.
  LOVE.

LOVE IS ENOUGH.

ARGUMENT.
  THIS story, which is told by way of a morality set before an Emperor and Empress newly wedded, showeth of a King whom nothing but Love might satisfy, who left all to seek Love, and, having found it, found this also, that he had enough, though he lacked all else.
  In the streets of a great town where the people are gathered together thronging to see the Emperor and Empress pass.
  GILES.
  L
  OOK long, Joan, while I hold you so, For the silver trumpets come arow.
  JOAN.
  O the sweet sound ! the glorious sight! O Giles, Giles, see this glittering Knight!
  B
  LOVE IS ENOUGH.
  GILES.
  Nay 'tis the Marshalls'-sergeant, sweet— — Hold, neighbour, let me keep my feet! — There, now your head is up again; Thus held up have you aught of pain ?
  JOAN.
  Nay, clear I see, and well at ease! God's body! what fair Kings be thes*e ?
  GILES.
  The Emperor's chamberlains, behold
  Their silver shoes and staves of gold.
  Look, look ! how like some heaven come down
  The maidens go with girded gown !
  JOAN.
  Yea, yea, and this last row of them Draw up their kirtles by the hem, And scatter roses e'en like those About my father's garden-close.
  GILES.

Ah ! have I hurt you ? See the girls Whose slim hands scatter very pearls,

LOVE IS ENOUGH.

JOAN.

Hold me fast, Giles ! here comes one Whose raiment flashes down the sun.

GILES.

O sweet mouth ! O fair lids cast down ! O white brow ! O the crown, the crown !

JOAN.

How near! if nigher I might stand By one ell, I could touch his hand.

GILES.

Look, Joan ! if on this side she were Almost my hand might touch her hair.

JOAN. Ah me ! what is she thinking on ?

GILES. Is he content now all is won ?

JOAN.

And does she think as I thought, when Betwixt the dancing maids and men,

LOVE IS ENOUGH.

'Twixt the porch rose-boughs blossomed red I saw the roses on my bed ?

GILES.

Hath he such fear within his heart As I had, when the wind did part The jasmine-leaves, and there within The new-lit taper glimmered thin ?

LOVE IS ENOUGH.

THE MUSIC (As the Emperor and Empress enter.)

LOVE is ENOUGH : though the World be a-waning_ And the woods have no voice but the voice of complaining,

Though the sky be too dark for dim eyes to discover The gold-cups and daisies fair blooming thereunder, 1 hough the hills be held shadows, and the sea a dark wonder,

And this day draw a veil over all deeds passed over, Yet their hands shall not tremble, their feet shall not falter; The void shall not weary, the fear shall not alter

These lips and these eyes of the loved and the lover.

LOVE IS ENOUGH.

THE EMPEROR.

THE spears flashed by me, and the swords swept round, And in war's hopeless tangle was I bound, But straw and stubble were the cold points found, For still thy hands led down the weary way.

THE EMPRESS.

Through hall and street they led me as a queen, They looked to see me proud and cold of mien, I heeded not though all my tears were seen, For still I dreamed of thee throughout the day.

THE EMPEROR.

Wild over bow and bulwark swept the sea Unto the iron coast upon our lee, Like painted cloth its fury was to me, For still thy hands led down the weary way.

THE EMPRESS.

They spoke to me of war within the land, They bade me sign defiance and command; I heeded not though thy name left my hand, For still I dreamed of thee throughout the day.

LOVE IS ENOUGH.

THE EMPEROR.

But now that I am come, and side by side We go, and men cry gladly on the bride And tremble at the image of my pride, Where is thy hand to lead me down the way?

THE EMPRESS.

But now that thou art come, and heaven and earth Are laughing in the fulness of their mirth, A shame I knew not in my heart has birth— —Draw me through dreams unto the end of day !

THE EMPEROR.

Behold, behold, how weak my heartJs_growji Now alLthe^heatof its desire is known ! Pearl beyond price I fear to call mine own, Where is thy hand to lead me down the way?

THE EMPRESS.

Behold, behold, how little I may move ! Think in thyjieart how terrible is Love, O thou who know'st my soul as God above— — Draw me through dreams unto the end of day !

LOVE IS ENOUGH.

The stage for the play in another part of the street, and the people thronging all about.

GILES.

HERE, Joan, this is so good a place Tis worth the scramble and the race ! There is the Empress just sat down, Her white hands on her golden gown, While yet the Emperor stands to hear The welcome of the bald-head Mayor Unto the show; and you shall see The player-folk come in presently. The king of whom is e'en that one, Who wandering but a while agone Stumbled upon our harvest-home That August when you might not come. Betwixt the stubble and the grass Great mirth indeed he brought to pass. But liefer were I to have seen Your nimble feet tread down the green In threesome dance to pipe and fife.

JOAN. Thou art a dear thing to my life,

And nought good have I far to seek — But hearken ! for the Mayor will speak.

THE MAYOR.

Since your grace bids me speak without stint or sparing

A thing little splendid I pray you to see :

Early is the day yet, for we near the dawning

Drew on chains dear-bought, and gowns done with gold;

So may ye high ones hearken an hour

A tale that our hearts hold worthy and good,

Of Pharamond the Freed, who, a king feared and honoured,

Fled away to find love from his crown and his folk.

E'en as I tell of it somewhat I tremble

Lest we, fearful of treason to the love that fulfils you,

Should seem to make little of the love that ye give us,

Of your lives full of glory, of the deeds that your lifetime

Shall gleam with for ever when we are forgotten.

Forgive it for the greatness of that Love who compels us.—

Hark ! in the minster-tower minish the joy-bells,

And all men are hushed now these marvels to hear.

THE EMPEROR (to the Mayor).

We thank your love, that sees our love indeed Toward you, toward Love, toward life of toil and need : We shall not falter though your poet sings

Of all defeat, strewing the crowns of kings | About the thorny ways where Love doth wend, / Because we know us faithful to the end

Toward you, toward Love, toward life of war and deed, And well we deem your tale shall help our need.

(To the Empress?)

So many hours to pass before the sun Shall blush ere sleeping, and the day be done ! How thinkest thou, my sweet, shall such a tale For lengthening or for shortening them avail ?

THE EMPRESS.

Nay, dreamland has no clocks the wise ones say, And while our hands move at the break of day We dream of years : and I am dreaming still And need no change my cup of joy to fill: Let them say on, and I shall hear thy voice Telling the tale and in its love rejoice.

LOVE IS ENOUGH.

THE MUSIC

(As the singers enter and stand before the curtain, the player-king and player-maiden in the midst.)

LOVE is ENOUGH : have no thought for to-morrow If ye lie down this even in rest from your pain,

Ye who have paid for your bliss with great sorrow ; For as it was once so it shall be again. Ye shall cry out for death as ye stretch forth in vain

Feeble hands to the hands that would help but they may not, Cry out to deaf ears that would hear if they could;

Till again shall the change come, and words your lips say not Your hearts make all plain in the best wise they would And the world ye thought waning is glorious and good :

And no morning now mocks you and no nightfall is weary, The plains are not empty of song and of deed:

The sea strayeth not, nor the mountains are dreary; The wind is not helpless for any maris need, Nor falleth the rain but for thistle and weed.

O surely this morning all sorrow is hidden, All battle zs hushed for this even at least;

And no one this noontide may hunger; unbidden

To the flowers and the singing and the joy of your feast Where silent ye sit midst the world's tale increased.

Lo, the lovers unloved that draw nigh for your blessing 7 For your tale makes the dreaming whereby yet they live

The dreams of the day with their hopes of redressing, The dreams of the night with the kisses they give, The dreams of the dawn wherein death and hope strive.

Ah, what shall we say then, but that earth threatened often Shall live on for ever that such things may be,

That the dry seed shall quicken, the hard earth shall soften, And the spring-bearing birds flutter north o'er the sea, That earth's garden may bloom round my love's feet and me ?

LOVE IS ENO UGH. 13

THE EMPEROR.

LO you, my sweet, fair folk are one and all And with good grace their broidered robes do fall, And sweet they sing indeed : but he, the King, Look but a little how his fingers cling To her's, his love that shall be in the play — His love that hath been surely ere to-day : And see, her wide soft eyes cast down at whiles Are opened not to note the people's smiles But her love's lips, and dreamily they stare As though they sought the happy country, where They two shall be alone, and the world dead.

THE EMPRESS.

Most faithful eyes indeed look from the head The sun has burnt, and wind and rain has beat, Well may he find her slim brown fingers sweet. And he — methinks hejrembles, lest he find That song of his not wholly to her mind. Note how his grey eyes look askance to see Her bosom heaving with the melody His heart loves well : rough with the wind and rain His cheek is, hollow with some ancient pain ; The sun has burned and blanched his crispy hair,

And over him hath swept a world of care
And left him careless, rugged, and her own ;
Still fresh desired, still strange and new, though known.

THE EMPEROR.

His eyes seem dreaming of the mysteries Deep in the depths of her familiar eyes, Tormenting and alluring; does he dream, As I ofttime this morn, how they would seem Loved but unloving?—Nay the world's too sweet That we the ghost of such a pain should meet— Behold, she goes, and he too, turning round, Remembers that his love must yet be found, That he is King and loveless in this story Wrought long ago for some dead poet's glory.

[Exeuntplayers behind the curtain.

Enter before the curtain LOVE crowned as a King.

LOVE.

ALL hail, my servants ! tremble ye, my foes ! A hope for these I have, a fear for those Hid in this tale of Pharamond the Freed. To-day, my Faithful, nought shall be your need Of tears compassionate :—although full oft The crown of love laid on my bosom soft Be woven of bitter death and deathless fame, Bethorned with woe, and fruited thick with shame. —This for the mighty of my courts I keep, Lest through the world there should be none to weep Except for sordid loss; and nought to gain But satiate pleasure making mock of pain. —Yea, in the heaven from whence my dreams go forth Are stored the signs that make the world of worth : There is the wavering wall of mighty Troy About my Helen's hope and Paris' joy: There lying neath the fresh dyed mulberry-tree The sword and cloth of Pyramus I see : There is the number of the joyless days Wherein Medea won no love nor praise : There is the sand my Ariadne pressed;

The footprints of the feet that knew no rest
While o'er the sea forth went the fatal sign :
The asp of Egypt, the Numidian wine,
My Sigurd's sword, my Brynhild's fiery bed,
The tale of years of Gudrun's drearihead,
And Tristram's glaive, and Iseult's shriek are here,
And cloister-gown of joyless Guenevere.
Save you, my Faithful! how your loving eyes
Grow soft and gleam with all these memories !
But on this day my crown is not of death :
My fire-tipped arrows, and my kindling breath
Are all the weapons I shall need to-day.
Nor shall my tale in measured cadence play
About the golden lyre of Gods long gone,
Nor dim and doubtful 'twixt the ocean's moan
Wail out about the Northern fiddle-bow,
Stammering with pride or quivering shrill with woe.
Rather caught up at hazard is the pipe
That mixed with scent of roses over ripe,
And murmur of the summer afternoon,
May charm you somewhat with its wavering tune

'Twixt joy and sadness : whatsoe'er it saith,
I know at least there breathes through it my breath.

OF PHARAMOND THE FREED.

Scene: In the Kings Chamber of Audience. MASTER OLIVER and many LORDS and COUNCILLORS.

A COUNCILLOR.

FAIR Master Oliver, thou who at all tiroes Mayst open thy heart to our lord and master, Tell us what tidings thou hast to deliver; For our hearts are grown heavy, and where shall we turn to If thus the king's glory, our gain and salvation, Must go down the wind amid gloom and despairing ?

MASTER OLIVER.
Little may be looked for, fair lords, in my story,
To lighten your hearts of the load lying on them.
For nine days the king hath slept not an hour,
And taketh no heed of soft words or beseeching.
Yea, look you, my lords, if a body late dead
In the lips and the cheeks should gain some little colour,
And arise and wend forth with no change in the eyes,
And wander about as if seeking its soul—
c
Lo, e'en so sad is my lord and my master; Yea, e'en so far hath his soul drifted from us.
A COUNCILLOR.
What say.the leeches ? Is all their skill left them?
MASTER OLIVER.
Nay, they bade lead him to hunt and to tilting,
To set him on high 'n the throne of his honour
To judge heavy deeds : bade him handle the tiller,
And drive through the sea with the wind at its wildest ;
All things he was wont to hold kingly and good.
So we led out his, steed and he straight leapt upon him
With no word, and no looking to right nor to left,
And into the forest we fared as aforetime:
Fast on the king followed, and cheered without stinting

The hcrfmds to the strife till the bear stood at bay; Then there he alone by the beech-trees alighted ; Barehanded, unarmoured, he handled the spear-shaft, And blew up the death on the horn of his father; Yet still in his eyes was no look of rejoicing, And no life in his lips ; but I likened him rather To King Nimrod carved fair on the back of the high-seat When the candles are dying, and the high moon is streaming Through window and luffer white on the lone pavement

Whence the guests are departed in the hall of the palace.Rode we home heavily, he with his rein loose, Feet hanging free from the stirrups, and staring At a clot of the bear's blood that stained his green kirtle ;Unkingly, unhappy, he rode his ways homeward.

A COUNCILLOR.
Was this all ye tried, or have ye more tidings ? For the wall tottereth not at first stroke of the ram.

MASTER OLIVER.

Nay, we brought him a-board the Great Dragon one dawning,
When the cold bay was flecked with the crests of white billows
And the clouds lay alow on the earth and the sea;
He looked not aloft as they hoisted the sail,
But with hand on the tiller hallooed to the shipmen
In a voice grown so strange, that it scarce had seemed stranger
If from the ship Argo, in seemly wise woven
On the guard-chamber hangings, some early grey dawning
Great Jason had cried, and his golden locks wavered.
Then e'en as the oars ran outboard, and dashed
In the wind-scattered foam and the sails bellied out,
His hand dropped from the tiller, and with feet all uncertain
And dull eye he wended him down to the midship,
And gazing about/or the place of the gangway
Made for the gate of the bulwark half open,
And stood there and stared at the swallowing sea,
Then turned, and uncertain went wandering back sternward,
And sat down on the deck by the side of the helmsman,
Wrapt in dreams of despair; so I bade them turn shoreward,
And slowly he rose as the side grated stoutly
'Gainst the stones of the quay and they cast forth the hawser.-
Unkingly, unhappy, he went his ways homeward.
A COUNCILLOR.
But by other ways yet had thy wisdom' to travel; How else did ye work for the winning
him peace ?
MASTER OLIVER.
We bade gather the knights for the goodliest tilting,
There the ladies went lightly in glorious array;
In the old arms we armed him whose dints well he knew
That the night dew had dulled and the sea salt had sullied :
On the old roan yet sturdy we set him astride;
So he stretched forth his hand to lay hold of the spear
Neither laughing nor frowning, as lightly his wont was
When the knights are awaiting the voice of the trumpet.
It awoke, and back beaten from barrier to barrier
Was caught up by knights' cries, by the cry of the king.—
—Such a cry as red Mars in the Council-room window
May awake with some noon when the last horn is winded, And the bones of the world are dashed grinding together. So it seemed to my heart, and a horror came o'er me, As the spears met, and splinters flew high o'er the field, And I saw the king stay when his course was at swiftest His horse straining hard on the bit, and he standing Stiff and stark in his stirrups, his spear held by the midmost, His helm cast a-back, his teeth set hard together ; E'en as one might, who, riding to heaven, feels round him The devils unseen : then he raised up the spear As to cast it away, but therewith failed his fury, He dropped it, and faintly sank back in the saddle, And, turning his horse from the press and the turmoil, Came sighing to me, and sore grieving I took him And led him away, while the lists were fallen silent As a fight in a dream that the light

breaketh through.— To the tune of the clinking of his fight-honoured armour Unkingly, unhappy, he went his ways homeward.

A COUNCILLOR.

What thing worse than the worst in the budget yet lieth?

MASTER OLIVER.

To the high court we brought him, and bade him to hearken The pleading of his people, and pass sentence on evil

His face changed with great pain, and his brow grew all furrowed,
As a grim tale was told there of the griefs of the lowly;
Till he took up the word, mid the trembling of tyrants,
As his calm voice and cold wrought death on ill doers—
— E'en so might King Minos in marble there carven
Mid old dreaming of Crete give doom on the dead,
When the world and its deeds are dead too and buried.—
But lo, as I looked, his clenched hands were loosened,
His lips grew all soft, and his eyes were beholding
Strange things we beheld not about and above him.
So he sat for a while, and then swept his robe round him
And arose and departed, not heeding his people,
The strange looks, the peering, the rustle and whisper;
But or ever he gained the gate that gave streetward,
Dull were his eyes grown, his feet were grown heavy,
His lips crooned complaining, as onward he stumbled ;—
Unhappy, unkingly, he went his ways homeward.

A COUNCILLOR.

Is all striving over then, fair Master Oliver ?

MASTER OLIVER.

All mine, lords, for ever ! help who may help henceforth I am but helpless : too surely meseemeth He seeth me not, and knoweth no more

Me that have loved him. Woe worth the while, Pharamond,
That men should love aught, love always as I loved !
Mother and sister and the sweetling that scorned me,
The wind of the autumn-tide over them sweepeth,
All are departed, but this one, the dear one—
I should die or he died and be no more alone,
But God's hatred hangs round me, and the life and the glory
That grew with my waning life fade now before it,
And leaving no pity depart through the void.

A COUNCILLOR.

This is a sight full sorry to see
These tears of an elder ! But soft now, one cometh.

MASTER OLIVER.

The feet of the king: will ye speak or begone ?

A NORTHERN LORD.

I will speak at the least, whoever keeps silence,
For well it may be that the voice of a stranger

Shall break through his dreaming better than thine;
And lo now a word in my mouth is a-coming,
That the king well may hearken : how sayst thou, fair master,
Whose name now I mind not, wilt thou have me essay it?
MASTER OLIVER.
Try whatso thou wilt, things may not be worser. [Enter KING. Behold, how he cometh weighed down by his woe!
(To the KING.)
All hail, lord and master! wilt thou hearken a little These lords high in honour whose hearts are full heavy Because thy heart sickeneth and knoweth no joy? —
(To the COUNCILLORS.)
Ah, see you ! all silent, his eyes set and dreary, His lips moving a little—how may I behold it?
THE NORTHERN LORD.
May I speak, king ? dost hearken ? many matters I have To deal with or death. I have honoured thee duly Down in the north there; a great name I have held thee; Rough hand in the field, ready righter of wrong, Reckless of danger, but recking of pity. But now—is it false what the chapmen have told us, And are thy fair robes all thou hast of a king ? Is it bragging and lies, that thou beardless and tender Weptst not when they brought thy slain father before thee, Trembledst not when the leaguer that lay round thy city Made a light for these windows, a noise for thy pillow ? Is it lies what men told us of thy singing and laughter
As thou layst in thy lair fled away from lost battle ?
Ts it lies how ye met in the depths of the mountains,
And a handful rushed down and made nought of an army ?
Those tales of your luck, like the tide at its turning,
Trusty and sure howso slowly it cometh,
Are they lies ? Is it lies of wide lands in the world,
How they sent thee great men to lie low at thy footstool
In five years thenceforward, and thou still a youth ?
Are they lies, these fair tidings, or what see thy lords here —
Some love-sick girl's brother caught up by that sickness,
As one street beggar catches the pest from his neighbour ?
KING PHARAMOND.
What words are these of lies and love-sickness ? Why am I lonely among all this brawling ?
0 foster-father, is all faith departed
That this hateful face should be staring upon me ?
THE NORTHERN LORD.
-Lo, now thou awakest; so tell me in what wise
1 shall wend back again : set a word in my mouth
To meet the folks' murmur, and give heart to the heavy; For there man speaks to man that thy measure is full, And thy five-years-old kingdom is falling asunder.
[KING draws his sword.
Yea, yea, a fair token thy sword were to send them; Thou dost well to draw it; (KING brandishes his sword over the load's head, as if to strike him) : soft sound is its whistle; Strike then, O king, for my wars are well over, And dull is the way my feet tread to the grave!

KING PHARAMOND (sheathing his sword].

Man, if ye have waked me, I bid you be wary

Lest my sword yet should reach you; ye wot in your northland

What hatred he winneth who waketh the shipman

From the sweet rest of death mid the welter of waves;

So with us may it fare; though I know thee full faithful

Bold in field and in council, most fit for a king.

—Bear with me. I pray you that to none may be meted

Such a measure of pain as my soul is oppressed with.

Depart all for a little, till my spirit_grows lighter,

Then come ye with tidings, and hold we fair council,

That my countries may know they have yet got a king.

[Exeunt all but OLIVER and KING. Come, my foster-father, ere thy visage fade from me, Come with me mid the flowers some opening to find In the clouds that cling round me; if thou canst remember Thine old lovingkindness when I was a king.

LOVE IS ENOUGH.

27

THE MUSIC.

LOVE is ENOUGH : it grew up without heeding

In the days when ye knew not its name nor its measure. And its leaflets untrodden by the light feet of pleasure

Had no boast of the blossom, no sign of the seeding, As the morning and evening passed over its treasure.

And what do ye say then ? — that Spring long departed Has brought forth no child to the softness and showers;

That we slept and we dreamed through the Summer of flowers;

We dreamed of the Winter, and waking dead-hearted Found Winter upon us and waste of dull hours.

Nay, Spring was der happy and knew not the reason,

And Slimmer dreamed sadly, for she thought all was ended In her fulness of wealth that might not be amended;

But this is the harvest and the garnering season,

And the leaf and the blossom in the ripe fruit are blended.

It sprang without sowing, it grew without heeding, Ye knew not its name and ye knew not its measure, Ye noted it not mid your hope and your pleasure ;

There was pain in its blossom, despair in its seeding. But daylong your bosom now nurseth its treasure.

Enter before the curtain LOVE clad as an image-maker. LOVE.

HOW mighty and how fierce a king is here The stayer of falling folks, the bane of fear ! Fair life he liveth, ruling passing well, Disdaining praise of Heaven and hate of Hell; And yet how goodly to us Great in Heaven Are such as he, the waning world that leaven! How well it were that such should never die ! How well it were at least that memory Of such should live, as live their glorious deeds !

— But which of all the Gods think ye it needs To shape the mist of Rumour's wavering breath Into a golden dream that fears no death ?

Red Mars belike? — since through his field is thrust The polished plough-share o'er the helmets' rust ! — Apollo's beauty ?— surely eld shall spare Smooth skin, and flashing eyes, and crispy hair! — Nay, Jove himself?—the pride that holds the low Apart, despised, to mighty tales must grow! — Or Pallas?—for the world that knoweth nought, By that great wisdom to the wicket brought, Clear through the tangle evermore shall see !

— O Faithful, O Beloved, turn to ME !

LOVE IS ENOUGH.

29

I am the Ancient of the Days that were, I am the Newborn that To-day brings here, I am the Life of all that dieth not; Through me alone is sorrow unforgot.

My Faithful, knowing that this man should live, I from the cradle gifts to him did give Unmeet belike for rulers of the earth; As sorrowful yearning in the midst of mirth, Pity midst anger, hope midst scorn and hate, Languor midst labour, lest the day wax late, And all be wrong, and all be to begin. Through these indeed the eager life did win That was the very body to my soul; Yet, as the tide of battle back did roll Before his patience : as he toiled and grieved O'er fools and folly, was he not deceived, But ever knew the change was drawing nigh, And in my mirror gazed with steadfast eye. Still, O my Faithful, seemed his life so fair That all Olympus might have left him there Until to bitter strength that life was grown, And then have smiled to see him die alone,

Had I not been. Ye know me ; I have sent

A pain to pierce his last coat of content:

Now must he tear the armour from his breast

(And cast aside all things that men deem best, And single-hearted for his longing strive That he at last may save his soul alive.

How say ye then, Beloved ? Ye have known The blossom of the seed these hands have sown Shall this man starve in sorrow's thorny brake ? Shall Love the faithful of his heart forsake ?

In the King's Garden. KING PHARAMOND, MASTER OLIVER.

MASTER OLIVER.

IN this quiet place canst thou speak, O my King, Where nought but the lilies may hearken our counsel ?

KING PHARAMOND.

What wouldst thou have of me? why came we hither?

MASTER OLIVER.

Dear lord, thou wouldst speak of the woe that weighs on thee.

KING PHARAMOND.

Wouldst thou bear me aback to the strife and the battle ? Nay, hang up my banner: 'tis all passed and over!

MASTER OLIVER.

Speak but a little, lord ! have I not loved thee ?

KING PHARAMOND.

Yea,—thou art Oliver : I saw thee a-lying

A long time ago with the blood on thy face,

When my father wept o'er thee for thy faith and thy valour.

MASTER OLIVER.

Years have passed over, but my faith hath not failed me; Spent is my might, but my love not departed. Shall not lovejiel^—yea, look long in my eyes ! There is no more to see if thou sawest my heart.

KING PHARAMOND.

Yea, thou art Oliver, full of all kindness !

Have patience, for now is the cloud passing over—

Have patience and hearken—yet shalt thou be shamed.

MASTER OLIVER.

Thou shalt shine through thy shame as the sun through the haze

When the world waiteth gladly the warm day a-coming:

As great as thou seem'st now, I know thee for greater

Than thy deeds done and told of: one day I shall know thee :

Lying dead in my tomb I shall hear the world praising.

KING PHARAMOND.

Stay thy praise—let me speak, lest all speech depart from me. —There is a place in the world, a great valley That seems a green plain from the brow of the mountains, But hath knolls and fair dales when adown there thou goest: There are homesteads therein with gardens about them,

And fair herds of kine and grey sheep a-feeding,

And willow-hung streams wend through deep grassy meadows,

And a highway winds through them from the outer world coming:

Girthed about is the vale by a grey wall of mountains,

Rent apart in three places and tumbled together

In old times of the world when the earth-fires flowed forth :

And as you wend up these away from the valley

You think of the sea and the great world it washes;

But through two you may pass not, the shattered rocks shut them.

And up through the third there windeth a highway,

And its gorge is fulfilled by a black wood of yew-trees.

And I know that beyond, though mine eyes have not seen it,

A city of merchants beside the sea lieth.

I adjure thee, my fosterer, by the hand of my father, By thy faith without stain, by the days unforgotten, When I dwelt in thy house ere the troubles' beginning, By thy fair wife long dead and thy sword-smitten children, By thy life without blame and thy love without blemish, Tell me how, tell me when, that fair land I may come to ! Hide it not for my help, for my honour, but tell me, Lest my time and thy time be lost days and confusion !

MASTER OLIVER.

O many such lands ! — O my master, what ails thee ? Tell me again, for I may not remember.

D

— I prayed God give thee speech, and lo God hath given it — May God give me death ! if I dream not this evil..

KING PHARAMOND.

Said I not when thou knew'st it, all courage should fail thee ? But me—my heart fails not, I am Pharamond as ever. I shall seek and shall find—come help me, my fosterer! — Yet if thou shouldst ask for a sign from that country What have I to show thee—I plucked a blue milk-wort From amidst of the field where she wandered fair-footed— It was gone when I wakened—and once in my wallet I set some grey stones from the way through the forest — These were gone when I wakened — and once as I wandered A lock of white wool from a thorn-bush I gathered; It was gone when I wakened—the name of that country— Nay, how should I know it ?—but ever meseemeth 'Twas not in the southlands, for sharp in the sunset And sunrise the air is, and whiles I have seen it Amid white drift of snow—ah, look up, foster-father!

MASTER OLIVER.

O woe, woe is me that I may not awaken!

Or else, art thou verily Pharamond my fosterling,

The Freed and the Freer, the Wise, the World's Wonder ?

KING PHARAMOND.

Why fainteth thy great heart ? nay, Oliver, hearken, E'en such as I am now these five years I have been. Through five years of striving this dreamer and dotard Has reaped glory from ruin, drawn peace from destruction.

MASTER OLIVER.

Woe's me ! wit hath failed me, and all the wise counsel

I was treasuring up down the wind is a-drifting —

Yet what wouldst thou have there if ever thou find it ?

Are the gates of heaven there? is Death bound there and helpless

KING PHARAMOND.

Nay, thou askest me this not as one without knowledge, For thou know'st that my love in that land is abiding.

MASTER OLIVER.

Yea—woe worth the while—and all wisdom hath failed me : Yet if thou wouldst tell me of her, I will hearken Without mocking or mourning, if that may avail thee.

KING PHARAMOND.

Lo, thy face is grown kind—Thou rememberest the even When I first wore the crown after sore strife and mourning ?

MASTER OLIVER.

Who shall ever forget it ? the dead face of thy father, And thou in thy fight-battered armour above it, Mid the passion of tears long held back by the battle ; And thy rent banner o'er thee and the ring of men mail-clad, Victorious to-day, since their ruin but a spear-length Was thrust away from them.—Son, think of thy glory And e'en in such wise break the throng of these devils !

KING PHARAMOND.

Five years are passed over since in the fresh dawning

On the field of that fight I lay wearied and sleepless

Till slumber came o'er me in the first of the sunrise;

Then as there lay my body rapt away was my spirit,

And a cold and thick mist for a while was about me,

And when that cleared away, lo, the mountain-walled country

'Neath the first of the sunrise in e'en such a spring-tide

As the spring-tide our horse-hoofs that yestereve trampled :

By the withy-wrought gate of a garden I found me

'Neath the goodly green boughs of the apple full-blossomed;

And fulfilled of great pleasure I was as I entered

The fair place of flowers, and wherefore I knew not.

Then lo, mid the birds' song a woman's voice singing.

Five years passed away, in the first of the sunrise.

\He is silent brooding.

MASTER OLIVER.

God help us if God is !—for this man, I deemed him More a glory of God made man for our helping Than a man that should die : all the deeds he did surely, Too great for a man's life, have undone the doer.

KING PHARAMOND (rousing himself\'7d. Thou art waiting, my fosterer, till I tell of her singing And the words that she sang there : time was when I knew them; But too much of strife is about us this morning, And whiles I forget and whiles I remember.

[Falls a-musing again.

MASTER OLIVER.

But a nighfs dream undid him, and he died, and his kingdom

By unheard of deeds fashioned, was tumbled together;

By false men and fools to be fought for and ruined.

Such words shall my ghost see the chronicler writing

In the days that shall be:—ah—what wouldst thou, my fosterling ?

Knowest thou not how words fail us awaking

That we seemed to hear plain amid sleep and its sweetness ?

Nay, strive not, my son, rest awhile and be silent;

Or sleep while I watch thee : full fair is the garden,

Perchance mid the flowers thy sweet dream may find thee,

And thou shalt have pleasure and peace for a little.—

(Aside) And my soul shall depart ere thou wak'st peradventure.

KING PHARAMOND.

Yea, thou deemest me,mad : a dream thou mayst call it But not such a dream as thou knoVst of: nay, hearken ! For what manner of dream then is this that remembers The words that she sang on that morning of glory ;— O love, set a word in my'mouth for our meeting Cast thy sweet arms about me to stay my hearfs beating ! Ah, thy silence, thy silence ! nought shines on the darkness ! —O close serried throng of the days that I see not!

[Falls a-musing again.

MASTER OLIVER.

Thus the worse that shall be, the bad that is, bettereth. — Once more he is speechless mid evil dreams sunken.

KING PHARAMOND (speaking very low).

Hold silence, love, speak not of the sweet day departed Cling close to me, love, lest I waken sad-hearted!

[Louder to OLIVER.

Thou starest, my fosterer : what strange thing beholdst thou? A great king, a strong man, that thou knewest a child once : Pharamond the fair babe : Pharamond the warrior; Pharamond the king, and which hast thou feared yet ? And why wilt thou fear then this Pharamond the lover ?

LOVE IS ENOUGH.

Shall I fail of my love who failed not of my fame ? Nay, nay, I shall live for the last gain and greatest.

39

MASTER OLIVER.

I know not—all counsel and wit is departed, I wait for thy will; I will do it, my master.

KING PHARAMOND.

i Through the boughs of the garden I followed the singing

To a smooth space of sward : there the unknown desire

Of my soul I beheld,—wrought in shape of a woman. i

MASTER OLIVER.

O ye warders of Troy-walls, join hands through the darkness, Tell us tales of the Downfall, for we too are with you !

KING PHARAMOND.

As my twin sister, young of years was she and slender, Yellow blossoms of spring-tide her hands had been gathering, But the gown-lap that held them had fallen adown And had lain round her feet with the first of the singing; Now her singing had ceased, though yet heaved her bosom ' As with lips lightly parted and eyes of one seeking She stood face to face with the Love that she knew not, The love that she longed for and waited unwitting ;

She moved not, I breathed not—till lo, a horn winded, And she started, and o'er her came trouble and wonder, Came pallor and trembling; came a strain at my heart-strings As bodiless there I stretched hands toward her beauty, And voiceless cried out, as the cold mist swept o'er me. Then again clash of arms, and the morning watch calling, And the long leaves and great twisted trunks of the chesnuts, As I sprang to my feet and turned round to the trumpets And gathering of spears and unfolding of banners That first morn of my reign and my glory's beginning.

MASTER OLIVER.

O well were we that tide though the world was against us.

KING PHARAMOND.

Hearken yet!—through that whirlwind of danger and battle,

Beaten back, struggling forward, we fought without blemish

On my banner spear-rent in the days of my father,

On my love of the land and the longing I cherished

For a tale to be told when I, laid in the minster,

Might hear it no more; was it easy of winning,

Our bread of those days ? Yet as wild as the work was

Unforgotten and sweet in my heart was that vision,

And her eyes and her lips and her fair body's fashion

Blest all times of rest, rent the battle asunder,

Turned ruin to laughter and death unto dreaming j

.And again and thrice over again did I go there

Ere spring was grown winter : in the meadows I met rftr,

By the sheaves of the corn, by the down-falling apples,

Kind and calm, yea and glad, yet with eyes of one seeking.

—Ah the mouth of one waiting, ere all shall be over!—

But at last in the winter-tide mid the dark forest

Side by side did we wend down the pass : the wind tangled

Mid the trunks and black boughs made wild music about us,

But her feet on the scant snow and the sound of her breathing

Made music much better: the wood thinned, and I saw her,

As we came to the brow of the pass ; for the moon gleamed

Bitter cold in the cloudless black sky of the winter.
Then the world drew me back from my love, and departing
I saw her sweet serious look pass into terror
And her arms cast abroad—and lo, clashing of armour,
And a sword in my hand, and my mouth crying loud,
And the moon and cold steel in the doorway burst open
And thy doughty spear thrust through the throat of the foeman
My dazed eyes scarce saw—thou rememberest, my fosterer?
MASTER OLIVER.
Yea, Theobald the Constable had watched but unduly;
We were taken unwares, and wild fleeing there was
O'er black rock and white snow—shall such times come again, son ?
KING PHARAMOND.
Yea, fufl surely they shall; have them courage, my fosterer !-
Day came thronging on day, month thrust month aside,
Amid battle and strife and the murder of glory,
And still oft and oft to that land was I led
And still through all longing I young in Love's dealings,
Never called it a pain : though, the battle passed over,
The council determined, back again came my craving :
I knew not the pain, but I knew all the pleasure,
When now, as the clouds o'er my fortune were parting,
I felt myself waxing in might and in wisdom;
And no city welcomed the Freed and the Freer,
And no mighty army fell back before rumour
Of Pharamond's coming, but her heart bid me thither
And the blithest and kindest of kingfolk ye knew me.
Then came the high tide of deliverance upon us,
When surely if we in the red field had fallen
The stocks and the stones would have risen to avenge us.
— Then waned my sweet vision midst glory's fulfilment,
And still with its waning, hot waxed my desire :
And did ye not note then that the glad-hearted Pharamond
Was grown a stern man. a fierce king, it may be ?
Did ye deem it the growth of my manhood, the hardening
Of battle and murder and treason about me ?
Nay. nay, it was love's pain, first named and first noted When a long time went past, and
I might not behold her.
— Thou rememberest a year agone now, when the legate Of the Lord of the Waters
brought here a broad letter
Full of prayers for good peace and our friendship thenceforward—
— He who erst set a price on the lost head of Pharamond — How I bade him stand up on
his feet and be merry,
Eat his meat by my side and drink out of my beaker,
In memory of days when my meat was but little
And my drink drunk in haste between saddle and straw.

But lo ! midst of my triumph, as I noted the feigning

Of the last foeman humbled, and the hall fell a murmuring,

And blithely the horns blew, Be glad, spring prevaileth,

— As I sat there and changed not, my soul saw a vision : All folk faded away, and my love that I long for

Came with raiment a-rustling along the hall pavement,

Drawing near to the high-seat, with hands held out a little,

Till her hallowed eyes drew me a space into heaven,

And her lips moved to whisper, ' Come, love, for I weary !'

Then she turned and went from me, and I heard her feet falling

On the floor of the hall, e'en as though it were empty

Of all folk but us twain in the hush of the dawning.

Then again, all was gone, and I sat there a smiling

On the faint-smiling legate, as the hall windows quivered

With the rain of the early night sweeping across them.

Nought slept I that night, yet I saw her without sleeping :— Betwixt midnight and morn of that summer-tide was I Amidst of the lilies by her house-door to hearken If perchance in her chamber she turned amid sleeping : When lo, as the East 'gan to change, and stars faded Were her feet on the stairs, and the door opened softly, And she stood on the threshold with the eyes of one seeking, And there, gathering the folds of her gown to her girdle, Went forth through the garden and followed the highway, All along the green valley, and I ever beside her, Till the light of the low sun just risen was falling On her feet in the first of the pass — and all faded. Yet from her unto me had gone forth her intent, And I saw her face set to the heart of that city, And the quays where the ships of the outlanders come to, -And I said; She is seeking, and shall I not seek ? The sea is her prison wall; where is my prison ? —Yet I said : Here men praise me, perchance men may love me If I live long enough for my justice and mercy To make them just and merciful—one who is master Of many poor folk, a man pity moveth Love hath dealt with in this wise, no minstrel nor dreamer. The deeds that my hand might find for the doing Did desire undo them these four years of fight? And now time and fair peace in my heart have begotten

LOVE IS ENOUGH.

45

More desire and more pain, is the day of deeds done with Lo here for my part my bonds and my prison ! Then with hands holding praise, yet with fierce heart belike Did I turn to the people that I had delivered And the deeds of this year passed shall live peradventure ! But now came no solace of dreams in the night-tide From that day thenceforward; yet oft in the council, Mid the hearkening folk craving for justice or mercy, Mid the righting of wrongs and the staying of ruin, Mid the ruling a dull folk, who deemed all my kingship A thing due and easy as the dawning and sunset To the day that God made once to deal with no further Mid all these a fair face, a sad face, could I fashion, And I said, She is seeking, and shall I not seek ? - Tell over the days of the year of hope's waning ; Tell over the hours of the weary days wearing : Tell over the minutes of the hours of thy waking, Then wonder he liveth who fails of his longing !

MASTER OLIVER.

What wouldst thou have, son, wherein I might help thee ?

KING PHARAMOND.

Hearken yet:—for a long time no more I beheld her Till a month agone now at the ending of Maytide;

And then in the first of the morning I found me
Fulfilled of all joy at the edge of the yew-wood;
Then lo, her gown's flutter in the fresh breeze of morning,
And slower and statelier than her wont was aforetime
And fairer of form toward the yew-wood she wended.
But woe's me ! as she came and .at last was beside me
With sobbing scarce ended her bosom was heaving,
Stained with tears was her face, and her mouth was yet quivering
With torment of weeping held back for a season.
Then swiftly my spirit to the King's bed was wafted
While still toward the sea were her weary feet wending.
—Ah surely that day of all wrongs that I hearkened
Mine own wrongs seemed heaviest and hardest to bear—
Mine own wrongs and hers—till that past year of ruling
Seemed a crime and a folly. Night came, and I saw her
Stealing barefoot, bareheaded amidst of the tulips
Made grey by the moonlight: and a long time Love gave me
To gaze on her weeping—morn came, and I wakened—
I wakened and said; Through the World will I wander,
fill either I find her, or find the World empty.
MASTER OLIVER.

Yea, son, wilt thou go ? Ah thou knowest from of old time My words might not stay thee from aught thou wert willing; And e'en so it must be now. And yet hast thou asked me

To go with thee, son, if aught I might help thee ?— —Ah me, if thy face might gladden a little I should meet the world better and mock, at its mocking: If thou goest to find her, why then hath there fallen This heaviness on thee ? is thy heart waxen feeble ?

KING PHARAMOND.
O friend, I have seen her no more, and her mourning
Is alone and unhelped—yet to-night or to-morrow
Somewhat nigher will I be to her love and her longing.
Lo, to thee, friend, alone of all folk on the earth
These things have I told: for a true man I deem thee
Beyond all men call true j yea, a wise man moreover
And hardy and helpful; and I know thy heart surely
That thou holdest the world nought without me thy fosterling.
Come, leave all awhile ! it may be as time weareth
With new life in our hands we shall wend us back hither.
MASTER OLIVER.

Yea; triumph turns trouble, and all the world changeth, Yet a good world it is since we twain are together.

KING PHARAMOND.

Lo, have I not said it?—thou art kinder than all men. Cast about then, I pray thee, to find us a keel

Sailing who recketh whither, since the world is so wide. Sure the northlands shall know of the blessings she bringeth And the southlands be singing of the tales that foretold her.

MASTER OLIVER.

Well I wot of all chapmen—and to-night weighs a dromond Sailing west away first, and then to the southlands. Since in such things I deal oft they know me, but know not King Pharamond the Freed, since now first they sail hither. So make me thy messenger in a fair-writ broad letter And thyself make my scrivener, and this very night sail we.— O surely thy face now is brightening and blesseth me! Peer through these boughs toward the bay and the haven, And high masts thou shalt see, and white sails hanging ready.

[Exit OLIVER.

KING PHARAMOND.

Dost thou weep now, my darling, and are thy feet wandering On the ways ever empty of what thou desirest ? Nay, nay, for thou know'st me, and many a night-tide Hath Love led thee forth to a city unknown : Thou hast paced through this palace from chamber to chamber Till in dawn and stars' paling I have passed forth before thee: Thou hast seen thine own dwelling nor known how to name it: Thine own dwelling that shall be when love is victorious.

Thou hast seen my sword glimmer amidst of the moonlight, As we rode with hoofs muffled through waylaying murder. Through the field of the dead hast thou fared to behold me, Seen me waking and longing by the watch-fires' flicker; Thou hast followed my banner amidst of the battle And seen my face change to the man that they fear Yet found me not fearful nor turned from beholding : Thou hast been at my triumphs, and heard the tale's ending Of my wars, and my winning through days evil and weary: For this eve hast thou waited, and wilt be peradventure By the sea-strand to-night, for thou wottest full surely That the word is gone forth, and the world is a-moving. —Abide me, beloved ! to-day and to-morrow Shall be little words in the tale of our loving, When the last morn ariseth, and thou and I meeting From lips laid together tell tales of these marvels.

THE MUSIC.

LOVE is ENOUGH : draw near and behold me

Ye who pass by the way to your rest and your laughter, And are full of the hope of the dawn coming after;

For the strong of the world have bought me and sold me

And my house is all wasted from threshold to rafter.

— Pass by me, and hearken, and think of me not!

Cry out and come near; for my ears may not hearken, And my eyes are grown dim as the eyes of the dying. Is this the grey rack o'er the surisface a-flying ?

Or is it your faces his brightness that darken ? Comes a wind from the sea, or is it your sighing? — Pass by me and hearken, and pity me not!

Ye know not how void is your hope and your living: Depart with your helping lest yet ye undo me! Ye know not that at nightfall she draweth near to me,

There is soft speech between us and words of forgiving Till in dead of the midnight her kisses thrill through me. — Pass by me and hearken, and waken me not!

Wherewith will ye buy it, ye rich who behold me ? Draw out from your coffers your rest and your laughter, And the fair gilded hope of the dawn coming after !

Nay this I sell not, — though ye bought me and sold me, —

For your house stored with such things from threshold to rafter. — Pass by me, I hearken, and think of you not!

Enter before the curtain LOVE clad as a Maker of Pictured Cloths.

LOVE.

THAT double life my faithful king has led My hand has untwined, and old days are dead

As in the moon the sails run up the mast. Yea, let this present mingle with the past, And when ye see him next think a long tide Of days are gone by; for the world is wide, And if at last these hands, these lips shall meet, What matter thorny ways and weary feet ?

A faithful king, and now grown wise in love :
Yet from of old in many ways I move
The hearts that shall be mine : him by the hand
Have I led forth, and shown his eyes the land
Where dwells his love, and shown him what she is:
He has beheld the lips that he shall kiss,
The eyes his eyes shall soften, and the cheek
His voice shall change, the limbs he maketh weak :
—All this he hath as in a picture wrought —
But lo you, 'tis the seeker and the sought:
For her no marvels of the night I make,
Nor keep my dream-smiths' drowsy heads awake;
LOVE IS ENOUGH.

53

Only about her have I shed a glory Whereby she waiteth trembling for a story That_she shall plavjn^—and 'tis not begun : Therefore from rising sun to setting sun There flit before her half-formed images Of what I am, and in all things she sees Something of mine : so single is her heart Filled with the worship of one set apart To be my priestess through all joy and sorrow; So sad and sweet she waits the certain morrow. —And yet sometimes, although her heart be strong, You may well think I tarry over-long: The lonely sweetness of desire grows pain, The reverent life of longing void and vain : Then are my dream-smiths mindful of my lore : They weave a web of sighs and weeping sore, Of languor, and of very helplessness, Of restless wandering, lonely dumb distress, Till like a live thing there she stands and goes, Gazing at Pharamond through all her woes. Then forth they fly, and spread the picture out Before his eyes, and how then may he doubt She knows his life, his deeds, and his desire ? How shall he tremble lest her heart should tire ? —It is not so; his danger and his war,

His days of triumph, and his years of care,
She knows them not—yet shall she know some day
The love that in his lonely longing lay.

What, Faithful—do I lie, that overshot My dream-web is with that which happeneth not ? Nay, nay, believe it not!—love lies alone In loving hearts like fire within the stone : >JZ | Then strikes my hand, and lo T thejlax ablaze ! —Those tales of empty striving, and lost days Folk tell of sometimes—never lit my fire Such ruin as this; but Pride and Vain-desire, My counterfeits and foes, have done the deed. Beware, beloved ! for they sow the weed Where I the wheat: they meddle where I leave, Take what I scorn, cast by what I receive, Sunder my yoke, yoke that I would dissever, Pull down the house my hands would build for ever

Scene: In a Forest among the Hills of a Foreign Land. KING PHARAMOND, MASTER OLIVER.

KING PHARAMOND,

QTRETCH forth thine hand, foster-father, I know thee, *^ And fain would be sure I am yet in the world : Where am I now, and what things have befallen ? Why am I so weary, and yet have wrought nothing ?

MASTER OLIVER.

Thou hast been sick, lord, but thy sickness abateth.

KING PHARAMOND.

Thou art sad unto weeping : sorry rags are thy raiment, For I see thee a little now : where am I lying ?

MASTER OLIVER.

On the sere leaves thou liest, lord, deep in the wild wood.

KING PHARAMOND.

What meaneth all this? was I not Pharamond, A worker of great deeds after my father, Freer of my land from murder and wrong, Fain of folks' love, and no blencher in battle ?

MASTER OLIVER.

Yea, thou wert king and the kindest under heaven.

KING PHARAMOND.

Was there not coming a Queen long desired, From a land over sea, my life to fulfil ?

MASTER OLIVER.

Belike it was so—but thou leftst it untold of.

KING PHARAMOND.

Why weepest thou more yet ? O me, which are dreams, Which are deeds of my life mid the things I remember ?

MASTER OLIVER.

Dost thou remember the great council chamber, O my king, and the lords there gathered together With drawn anxious faces one fair morning of summer, And myself in their midst, who would move thee to speech ?

KING PHARAMOND.

A brawl I remember, some wordy debating, Whether my love should be brought to behold me. Sick was I at heart, little patience I had.

MASTER OLIVER.

Hast thou memory yet left thee, how an hour thereafter
We twain lay together in the midst of the pleasance
'Neath the lime-trees, nigh the pear-tree, beholding the conduit ?

KING PHARAMOND.

Fair things I remember of a long time thereafter— Of thy love and thy faith and our gladness together.

MASTER OLIVER.

And the thing that we talked of, wilt thou tell me about it ?

KING PHARAMOND.

We twain_were^ tpjwend. through the wide world together Seeking myjove—O my heart! is she living?

MASTER OLIVER.

God wot that she liveth as she hath lived ever.

KING PHARAMOND.

Then soon was it midnight, and moonset, as we wended Down to the ship, and the merchant-folks' babble. The oily green waves in the harbour mouth glistened, Windless midnight it was, but the great sweeps were run out, As the cable came rattling mid rich bales on the deck, And slow moved the black side that the ripple was lapping,

And I looked and beheld a great city behind us
By the last of the moon as the stars were a-brightening,

And Pharamond the Freed grew a tale of a singer,
With the land of his fathers and the fame he had toiled for.
Yet sweet was the scent of the sea-breeze arising;
And I felt a chain broken, a sickness put from me
As the sails drew, and merchant-folk, gathered together
On the poop or the prow, 'gan to move and begone,
Till at last 'neath the far-gazing eyes of the steersman
By the loitering watch thou and I were left lonely,
And we saw by the moon the white horses arising
Where beyond the last headland the ocean abode us,
Then came the fresh breeze and the sweep of the spray,
And the beating of ropes, and the empty sails' thunder,
As we shifted our course toward the west in the dawning;
Then I slept and I dreamed in the dark I was lying,
And I heard her sweet breath and her feet falling near me,
And the rustle of her raiment as she sought through the darkness,
Sought, I knew not for what, till her arms clung about me
With a cry that was hers, that was mine as I wakened.
MASTER OLIVER.
Yea, a sweet dream it was, as thy dreams were aforetime.
KING PHARAMOND.
Nay not so, my fosterer: thy hope yet shall fail thee
Ir thou lookest tojsee me turned back from myjblly, Lamenting andjmocking the life of my longing. Many such have I had, dear dreams and deceitful, When the soul slept a little from all but its search, And lied to the body of bliss beyond telling; Yea, waking had lied still but for life and its torment. Not so were those dreams of the days of my kingship, Slept my body—or died—but my soul was not sleeping, It knew that she touched not this body that trembled At the thought of her body sore trembling to see me; It lied of no bliss as desire swept it onward, Who knows through what sundering space of its prison ; It saw, and it heard, and it hoped, and was lonely, Had no doubt and no joy, but the hope that endureth. —Woe's me I am weary: wend we forward to-morrow?

MASTER OLIVER.
Yea, well it may be if thou wilt but be patient, And rest thee a little, while time creepeth onward.

KING PHARAMOND.
But tell me, has the fourth year gone far mid my sickness ?
MASTER OLIVER.
Nay, for seven days only didst thou lie here a-dying,
As full often I deemed : God be thanked it is over !
But rest thee a little, lord; gather strength for the striving.
KING PHARAMOND.
Yea, for once again sleep meseems cometh to struggle With the memory of times past: come tell thou, my fosterer, Of the days we have fared through, that dimly before me Are floating, as I look on thy face and its trouble.

MASTER OLIVER.
Rememberest thou aught of the lands where we wended ?

KING PHARAMOND.

Yea, many a thing—as the moonlit warm evening When we stayed by the trees in the Gold-bearing Land, Nigh the gate of the city, where a minstrel was singing That tale of the King and his fate, o'er the cradle Foretold by the wise of the world; that a woman Should win him to love and to woe, and despairing In the last of his youth, the first days of his manhood.

MASTER OLIVER.

I remember the evening; but clean gone is the story: Amid deeds great and dreadful, should songs abide by me ?

KING PHARAMOND.

They shut the young king in a castle, the tale saith,
Where never came woman, and never should come,
And sadly he grew up and stored with all wisdom,
Not wishing for aught in his heart that he had not,
Till the time was come round to his twentieth birthday.
Then many fair gifts brought his people unto him,
Gold and gems, and rich cloths, and rare things and dear-bought,
And a book fairly written brought a wise man among them,
Called the Praising of Prudence; wherein there was painted
The image of Prudence :—and that, what but a woman,
E'en she forsooth that the painter found fairest;—
Now surely thou mindest what needs must come after?

MASTER OLIVER.

Yea, somewhat indeed I remember the misery
Told in that tale, but all mingled it is
With the manifold trouble that met us full often,
E'en we ourselves. Of nought else hast thou memory ?

KING PHARAMOND.

Of many such tales that the Southland folk told us,
Of many a dream by the sunlight and moonlight;
Of music that moved me, of hopes that my heart had;
The high days when my love and I held feast together. — But what land is this, and how came we hither?

MASTER OLIVER.

Nay, hast thou no memory of our troubles that were many ?
How thou criedst out for Death and how near Death came to thee?
How thou needs must dread war, thou the dreadful in battle ?
Of the pest in the place where that tale was told to us ;
And how we fled thence o'er the desert of horror ?
How weary we wandered when we came to the mountains,
All dead but one man of those who went with us ?
How we came to the sea of the west, and the city,
Whose Queen would have kept thee her slave and her lover,
And how we escaped by the fair woman's kindness,
Who loved thee, and cast her life by for thy welfare ?
Of the waste of thy life when we sailed from the Southlands,
And the sea-thieves fell on us and sold us for servants

To that land of hard gems, where thy life's purchase seemed
Little better than mine, and we found to our sorrow
Whence came the crown's glitter, thy sign once of glory:
Then naked a king toiled in sharp rocky crannies,
And thy world's fear was grown but the task-master's whip,
And thy world's hope the dream in the short dead of night ?
And hast thou forgotten how again we fled from it,
And that fight of despair in the boat on the river,
And the sea-strand again and white bellying sails;
And the sore drought and famine that on ship-board fell on us,
Ere the sea was o'erpast, and we came scarcely living
To those keepers of sheep,- the poor folk and the kind ?
Dost thou mind not the merchants who brought us thence northward,
And this land that we made in the twilight of dawning ?
And the city herein where all kindness forsook us,
And our bitter bread sought we from house-door to house-door

KING PHARAMOND.

As the shadow of clouds o'er the summer sea sailing
Is the memory of all now, and whiles I remember
And whiles I forget; and nought it availeth
Remembering, forgetting ; for a sleep is upon me
That shall last a long while :—there thou liest, my fosterer,
As thou lay'st a while since ere that twilight of dawning;
And I woke and looked forth, and the dark sea, long changeless,
Was now at last barred by a dim wall that swallowed
The red shapeless moon, and the whole sea was rolling,
Unresting, unvaried, as grey as the void is,
Toward that wall 'gainst the heavens as though rest were behind it.
Still onward we fared and the moon was forgotten,
And colder the sea grew and colder the heavens,
And blacker the wall grew, and grey, green-besprinkled,
And the sky seemed to breach it; and lo at the last
Many islands of mountains, and a city amongst them. White clouds of the dawn, not moving yet waning, Wreathed the high peaks about; and the sea beat for ever 'Gainst the green sloping hills and the black rocks and beachless.

— Is this the same land that I saw in that dawning ? For sure if it is thou at least shalt hear tidings, Though I die ere the dark : but for thee, O my fosterer, Lying there by my side, I had deemed the old vision Had drawn forth the soul from my body to see her.

And with joy and fear blended leapt the heart in my bosom, And I cried, ' The last land, love ; O hast thou abided ?' But since then hath been turmoil, and sickness, and slumber, And my soul hath been troubled with dreams that I knew not. And such tangle is round me life fails me to rend it, And the cold cloud of death rolleth onward to hide me.—

— O well am I hidden, who might not be happy! I see not, I hear not, my head groweth heavy.

[Falls back as if sleeping.

MASTER OLIVER.

—O Son, is it sleep that upon thee is fallen?

Not death, O my dear one !—speak yet but a little !

KING PHARAMOND (raising himself again). O be glad, foster-father! and those troubles past over,—

Be thou thereby when once more I remember
And sit with my maiden and tell her the story,
And we pity our past selves as a poet may pity
The poor folk he tells of amid plentiful weeping.
Hush now! as faint noise of bells over water
A sweet sound floats towards me, and blesses my slumber:
If I wake never more I shall dream and shall see her. [Sleeps.

MASTER OLIVER.

Is it swooning or sleeping ? in what wise shall he waken ? —Nay, no sound I hear save the forest wind wailing. Who shall help us today save our yoke-fellow Death ? Yet fain would I die mid the sun and the flowers ; For a tomb seems this yew-wood ere yet we are dead, And its wailing wind chilleth my yearning for time past, And my love groweth cold in this dusk of the daytime. What will be ? is worse than death drawing anear us ? Flit past, dreary day ! come, night-tide and resting ! Come, tomorrow's uprising with light and new tidings ! —Lo, Lord, I have borne all with no bright love before me; Wilt thou break all I had and then give me no blessing ?

THE MUSIC.

LOVE is ENOUGH : through the trouble and tangle From yesterdays dawning to yesterday's night

I sought through the vales where the prisoned winds wrangle, Till, wearied and bleeding, at end of the light I met him, and we wrestled, and great was my might.

O great was my joy, though no rest was around me,
Though mid wastes of the world were we twain all alone,
For methought that I conquered and he knelt and he crowned me, And the driving rain ceased, and the wind ceased to moan, And through clefts of the clouds her planet outshone.

O through clefts of the clouds 'gan the world to awaken, And the bitter wind piped, and down drifted the rain,
And I was alone — and yet not forsaken,
For the grass was untrodden except by my pain : With a Shadow of the Night had I wrestled in vain.

And the Shadow of the Night and not Love was departed; I was sore, I was weary, yet Love lived to seek ;

So scaled the dark mountains, and wandered sad-hearted Over wearier wastes, where Jen sunlight was bleak, With no rest of the night for my soul waxen weak.

With no rest of the night; for I waked mid a story Of a land wherein Love is the light and the lord,

Where my tale shall be heard, and my wounds gain a glory\ And my tears be a treasure to add to the hoard Of pleasure laid up for his people's reward.

Ah, pleasure laid up ! haste thou onward and listen, For the wind of the waste has no music like this,

And not thus do the rocks of the wilderness glisten : With the host of his faithful through sorrow and bliss My Lord go eth forth now, and knows me for his.

Enter before the curtain LOVE, with a cup of bitter drink and his hands bloody.

LOVE.

OPHARAMOND, I knew thee brave and strong, And yet how might'st thou live to bear this wrong ? — A wandering-tide of three long bitter years, Solaced at whiles by languor of soft tears, By dreams self-wrought of night and sleep and sorrow, Holpen by hope of tears to be tomorrow : Yet all, alas, but wavering memories; No vision of her hands, her lips, her eyes, Has blessed him since he seemed to see her weep, No wandering feet of hers beset his sleep.

Woe's me then! am I cruel, or am I grown The scourge of Fate, lest men forget to moan ? What!—is there blood upon these hands of mine ? Is venomed anguish mingled with my wine ? —Blood there may be, and venom in the cup ; But see, Beloved, how the tears well up From my grieved heart my blinded eyes to grieve, And in the kindness of old days believe!

So after all then we must weep today—
—We, who behold at ending of the way,
These lovers tread a bower they may not miss
Whose door my servant keepeth, Earthly Bliss :
There in a little while shall they abide,
Nor each from each their wounds of wandering hide,
But kiss them, each on each, and find it sweet,
That wounded so the world they may not meet.
—Ah, truly mine ! since this your tears may move,
The very sweetness of rewarded love !
Ah, truly mine, that tremble as ye hear
The speech of loving lips grown close and dear;
—Lest other sounds from other doors ye hearken,
Doors that the wings of Earthly Anguish darken.
Scene: On a Highway in a Valley near the last, with a Mist over all things.
KING PHARAMOND, MASTER OLIVER. KING PHARAMOND.

HOLD a while, Oliver! my limbs are grown weaker Than when in the wood I first rose to my feet. There was hope in my heart then, and now nought but sickness ; There was sight in my eyes then, and now nought but blindness. Good art thou, hope, while the life yet tormenteth, But a better help now have I gained than thy goading. Farewell, O life, wherein once I was merry! O dream of the world, I depart now, and leave thee A little tale added to thy long-drawn-out story. Cruel wert thou, O Love, yet have thou and I conquered. —Come nearer, O fosterer, come nearer and kiss me, Bid farewell to thy fosterling while the life yet is in me, For this farewell to thee is my last word meseemeth.

He lies down and sleeps.

MASTER OLIVER.

O my king, O my son ! Ah, woe's me for my kindness, For the day when thou drew'st me and I let thee be drawn
Into toils I knew deadly, into death thou desiredst!
And woe's me that I die not! for my body made hardy
By the battles of old days to bear every anguish !
—Speak a word and forgive me, for who knows how long yet
Are the days of my life, and the hours of my loathing!
He speaks not, he moves not: yet he draweth breath softly:
I have seen men a-dying, and not thus did the end come.

Surely God who made all forgets not love's rewarding,
Forgets not the faithful, the guileless who fear not.
Oh, might there be help yet, and some new life's beginning !
— Lo, lighter the mist grows: there come sounds through its dulness,
The lowing of kine, or the whoop of a shepherd,
The bell-wether's tinkle, or clatter of horse-hoofs.
A homestead is nigh us: I will fare down the highway
And seek for some helping: folk said simple people
Abode in this valley, and these may avail us—
If aught it avail us to live for a little.
—Yea, give it us, God !—all the fame and the glory
We fought for and gained once; the life of well-doing,
Fair deed thrusting on deed, and no day forgotten ;
And due worship of folk that his great heart had holpen;—
All I prayed for him once now no longer I pray for.
Let it all pass away as my warm breath now passeth
In the chill of the morning mist wherewith thou hidest
Fair vale and grey mountain of the land we are come to !

Let it all pass away! but some peace and some pleasure I pray for him yet, and that 1 may behold it. A prayer little and lowly,— and we in the old time When the world lay before us, were we hard to the lowly ? Thou know'st we were kind, howso hard to be beaten; Wilt thou help us this last time ? or what hast thou hidden We know not, we name not, some crown for our striving ? — O body and soul of my son, may God keep thee ! For, as lone as thou liest in a land that we see not When the world loseth thee, what is left for its losing ?

[Exit OLIVER.

THE MUSIC.

LOVE is ENOUGH : cherish life that abideth,

Lest ye die ere ye know him, and curse and misname him ; For who knows in what ruin of all hope he hideth, On what wings of the terror of darkness he rideth ?

And what is the joy of maris life that ye blame him For his bliss grown a sword, and his rest grown afire ?

Ye who tremble for death, or the death of desire, Pass about the cold winter-tide garden and ponder

On the rose in his glory amidst of 'June's fire,

On the languor of noontide that gathered the thunder, On the morn and its freshness, the eve and its wonder : Ye may wake it no more — shall Spring come to awaken ?

Live on, for Love liveth, and earth shall be shaken

By the wind of his wings on the triumphing morning, When the dead, and their deeds that die not shall awaken, And the world's tale shall sound in your trumpet of warning, And the sun smite the banner called Scorn of the Scorning, And dead pain ye shall trample, dead fruitless desire, As ye wend to pluck out the new world from the fire.

Enter before the curtain, LOVE clad as a Pilgrim.

LOVE.

ALONE, afar from home doth Pharamond lie, Drawn near to death, ye deem—or what draws nigh ? Afar from home—and have ye any deeming How far may be that country of his dreaming ? Is it not time, is it not time, say ye, That we the day-star in the sky should see ?

Patience, Beloved; these may come to live A life fulfilled of all I have to give, But bare of strife and story; and ye know well How wild a tale of him might be to tell Had I not snatched away the sword and crown; Yea, and she too was made for world's renown, And should have won it, had my bow not been; These that I love were very king and queen; I have discrowned them, shall I not crown too ? Ye know, Beloved, what sharp bitter dew, What parching torment of unresting day Falls on the garden of my deathless bay : Hands that have gathered it and feet that came Beneath its shadow have known flint and flame ;

Therefore I love them; and they love no less Each furlong of the road of past distress. — Ah, Faithful, tell me for what rest and peace, What length of happy days and world's increase, What hate of wailing, and what love of laughter, What hope and fear of worlds to be hereafter, Would ye cast by that crown of bitter leaves ?

And yet, ye say, our very heart it grieves To see him lying there : how may he save His life and love if he more pain must have ? And she—how fares it with her ? is not earth From winter's sorrow unto summer's mirth Grown all too narrow for her yearning heart ? We pray thee, Love, keep these no more apart.

Ye say but sooth: not long may he endure: And her heart sickeneth past all help or cure Unless I hasten to the helping—see, Am I not girt for going speedily ? —The journey lies before me long?—nay, nay, Upon my feet the dust is lying grey, The staff is heavy in my hand.—Ye too, Have ye not slept ? or what is this ye do, Wearying to find the country ye are in ?

The curtain draws up and shows the same scene as the last, with the mist clearing, and PHARAMOND lying there as before.

Look, look! how sun and morn at last do win Upon the shifting waves of mist! behold That mountain-wall the earth-fires rent of old, Grey toward the valley, sun-gilt at the side ! See the black yew-wood that the pass doth hide ! Search through the mist for knoll, and fruited tree, And winding stream, and highway white—and see, See, at my feet lies Pharamond the Freed ! A happy journey have we gone indeed !

Hearken, Beloved, over-long, ye deem,
I let these lovers deal with hope and dream
Alone unholpen.—Somewhat sooth ye say :
But now her feet are on this very way
That leadeth from the city: and she saith
One beckoneth her back hitherward — even Death —
And who was that, Beloved, but even I ?
Yet though her feet and sunlight are drawn nigh
The cold grass where he lieth like the dead,
To ease your hearts a little of their dread
I will abide her coming, and in speech
He knoweth, somewhat of his welfare teach.
H

LOVE IS ENOUGH. 7 7

LOVE goes on to the Stage and stands at PHARAMOND'S head.

LOVE. EARKEN, O Pharamond, why earnest thou hither ?

KING PHARAMOND.

I came seeking Death ; I have found him belike.

LOVE. In what land of the world art thou lying, O Pharamond?

KING PHARAMOND.

-In a land 'twixt two worlds : nor long shall I dwell there.

LOVE. Wfio am I, Pharamond, that stand here beside thee ?

KING PHARAMOND.

The Death I have sought—thou art welcome; I greet thee

LOVE. Such a name have I had, but another name have I.

KING PHARAMOND.

Art thou God then that helps not until the last season?

LOVE. Yea, God am I surely j yet another name have I.

KING PHARAMOND.

Methinks as I hearken, thy voice I should wot of.

LOVE. I called thee, and thou cam'st from thy glory and kingship.

KING PHARAMOND.

I was King Pharamond, and love overcame me.

LOVE. Pharamond, thou sa/st it.—I am Love and thy master.

KING PHARAMOND.

Sooth didst thou say when thou call'dst thyself Death.

LOVE. Though thou diest, yet thy love and thy deeds shall I quicken,

KING PHARAMOND.

Be thou God, be thou Death, yet I love thee and dread not.

LOVE. Pharamond, while thou livedst what thing wert thou loving ?

KING PHARAMOND.

A dream and a lie—and my death—and I love it.

LOVE. Pharamond, do my bidding, as thy wont was aforetime.

KING PHARAMOND.

What wilt thou have of me, for I wend away swiftly ?

LOVE. Open thine eyes, and behold where thou liest!

KING PHARAMOND.

It is little—the old dream, the old lie is about me.

LOVE. Why faintest thou, Pharamond ? is love then unworthy ?

KING PHARAMOND.

Then hath God made no world now, nor shall make hereafter.

LOVE.

Wouldst thou live if thou mightst in this fair world, O Pharamond ?

KING PHARAMOND.

Yea, if she and truth were; nay, if she and truth were not.

LOVE.

O long shalt thou live : thou art here in the body, Where nought but thy spirit I brought in days bygone. Ah, thou hearkenest!—and where then of old hast thou heard it?

[Music outside, far off.

KING PHARAMOND.

O mock me not, Death; or, Life, hold me no longer! For that sweet strain I hear that I heard once a-dreaming: Is it death coming nigher, or life come back that brings it ? Or rather my dream come again as aforetime ?

LOVE. Look up, O Pharamond! canst thou see aught about thee ?

KING PHARAMOND.

Yea, surely : all things as aforetime I saw them : The mist fading out with the first of the sunlight,

And the mountains a-changing as oft in my dreaming, And the thornbrake anigh blossomed thick with the May-tide.

[Music again. O my heart! — I am hearkening thee whereso thou wanderest!

LOVE. Put forth thine hand, feel the dew on the daisies !

KING PHARAMOND.

So their freshness I felt in the days ere hope perished. —O me, me, my darling! how fair the world groweth ! Ah, shall I not find thee, if death yet should linger, Else why grow I so glad now when life seems departing ? What pleasure thus pierceth my heart unto fainting ? — O me, into words now thy melody passeth.

MUSIC with singing (from without).

Dawn talks to-day

Over dew-gleaming flowers^ Night flies away

Till the resting of hours: Fresh are thy feet

And with dreams thine eyes glistening,

Thy stilllips are sweet

Though the world is a-listening. O Love, set a word in my mouth for our meeting, Cast thine arms round about me to stay my heart's beating / O fresh day, Ofair day, O long day made ours /

LOVE. What wilt thou say now of the gifts Love hath given ?

KING PHARAMOND.

Stay thy whispering, O wind of the morning—she speaketh.

THE MUSIC (coming nearer).

Morn shall meet noon

While the flower-stems yet move, Though the wind dieth soon And the clouds fade above. Loved lips are thine

As I tremble and hearken; Bright thine eyes shine,

Though the leaves thy brow darken. O Love, kiss me into silence, lest no word avail me, Stay my head with thy bosom lest breath and life fail me ! O sweet day, O rich day, made long for our love /

LOVE IS ENOUGH. 83

LOVE.

Was Love then a liar who fashioned thy dreaming ?

KING PHARAMOND.

O fair-blossomed tree, stay thy rustling—I hearken.

THE MUSIC (coming nearer).

Late day shall greet eve,

And the full blossoms shake, For the wind will not leave

The tall trees while they wake. Eyes soft with bliss,

Come nigher and Higher Sweet mouth I kiss,

Tell me all thy desire

Let us speak, love, together some words of our story, That our lips as they part may remember the glory f O soft day, O calm day, made clear for our sake !

LOVE.

What wouldst thou, Pharamond ? why art thou fainting ?

KING PHARAMOND.

And thou diest, fair daylight, now she draweth near me !
THE MUSIC (close outside).
Eve shall kiss night.
And the leaves stir like rain As the wind stealeth light
O'er the grass of the plain. Unseen are thine eyes
Mid the dreamy nighfs sleeping, And on my mouth there lies
The dear rain of thy weeping.
Hold silence, love, speak not of the sweet day departed, Cling close to me, love, lest I waken sad-hearted / O kind day, O dear day, short day, come again I
LOVE.
Sleep then, O Pharamond, till her kiss shall awake thee,
For, lo, here comes the sun o'er the tops of the mountains,
And she with his light in her hair comes before him,
As solemn and fair as the dawn of the May-tide
On some isle of mid-ocean when all winds are sleeping.
O worthy is she of this hour that awaits her,
And the death of all doubt, and beginning of gladness
Her great heart shall embrace without fear or amazement.
— He sleeps, yet his heart's beating measures her footfalls; And her heart beateth too, as her feet bear her onward: Breathe gently between them, O breeze of the morning! Wind round them unthought of, sweet scent of the blossoms ! Treasure up every minute of this tide of their meeting, O flower-bedecked Earth ! with such tales of my triumph Is your life still renewed, and spring comes back for ever From that forge of all glory that brought forth my blessing. O welcome, Love's darling ! Shall this day ever darken, Whose dawn I have dight for thy longing triumphant ?
[Exit Lo VE. Enter AZA LA is.
AZALAIS.
A song in my mouth, then ? my heart full of gladness ?
My feet firm on the earth, as when youth was beginning ?
And the rest of my early days come back to bless me ?—
Who hath brought me these gifts in the midst of the May-tide ?
What!—three days agone to the city I wandered,
And watched the ships warped to the Quay of the Merchants;
And wondered why folk should be busy and anxious;
For bitter my heart was, and life seemed a-waning,
With no story told, with sweet longing turned torment,
Love turned to abasement, and rest gone for ever.
And last night I awoke with a pain piercing through me,
And a cry in my ears, and Death passed on before, As one pointing the way, and I rose up sore trembling, And by cloud and by night went before the sun's coming, As one goeth to death,—and lo here the dawning ! And a dawning therewith of a dear joy I know not. I have given back the day the glad greeting it gave me; And the gladness it gave me, that too would I give
Were hands held out to crave it. Fair valley I greet thee,
And the new-wakened voices of all things familiar.
— Behold, how the mist-bow lies bright on the mountain, Bidding hope as of old since

no prison endureth.

Full busy has May been these days I have missed her, And the milkwort is blooming, and blue falls the speedwell. —Lo, here have been footsteps in the first of the morning, Since the moon sank all red in the mist now departed. —Ah ! what lieth there by the side of the highway? Is it death stains the sunlight, or sorrow or sickness ?

[Going up to PHARAMOND.

—Not death, for he sleepeth ; but beauty sore blemished By sorrow and sickness, and for all that the sweeter. I will wait till he wakens and gaze on his beauty, Lest I never again in the world should behold him.

— Maybe I may help him; he is sick and needs tending, He is poor, and shall scorn not our simpleness surely. Whence came he to us-ward—what like has his life been—

Who spoke to him last—for what is he longing?

—As one hearkening a story I wonder what cometh,

And in what wise my voice to our homestead shall bid him.

0 heart, how thou faintest with hope of the gladness

1 may have for a little if there he abide.

Soft there shalt thou sleep, love, and sweet shall thy dreams be,

And sweet thy awaking amidst of the wonder

Where thou art, who is nigh thee—and then, when thou seest

How the rose-boughs hang in o'er the little loft window,

And the blue bowl with roses is close to thine hand,

And over thy bed is the quilt sewn with lilies,

And the loft is hung round with the green Southland hangings,

And all smelleth sweet as the low door is opened,

And thou turnest to see me there standing, and holding

Such dainties as may be, thy new hunger to stay —

Then well may I hope that thou wilt not remember

Thine old woes for a moment in the freshness and pleasure,

And that I shall be part of thy rest for a little.

And then—who shall say—wilt thou tell me thy story,

And what thou hast loved, and for what thou hast striven ?

—Thou shalt see me, and my love and my pity, as thou speakest,

And it may be thy pity shall mingle with mine.

—And meanwhile Ah, love, what hope may my heart hold?

For I see that thou lovest, who ne'er hast beheld me.

And how should thy love change, howe'er the world changeth?

Yet meanwhile, had I dreamed of the bliss of this minute, How might I have borne to live weary and waiting !

Woe's me ! do I fear thee ? else should I not wake thee, For tending thou needest.— If my hand touched thy hand

[Touching htm.

I should fear thee the less.— O sweet friend, forgive it, My hand and my tears, for faintly they touched thee ! He trembleth, and waketh not: O me, my darling ! Hope whispers that thou hear'st me through sleep, and wouldst waken But for dread that thou dreamest and I should be gone. Doth it please thee in dreaming that I tremble and dread thee, That these tears are the tears of one praying vainly, Who shall pray with no word when thou hast awakened ? —Yet how shall

I deal with my life if he love not, As how should he love me, a stranger, unheard of? — O bear witness, thou day that hast brought my love hither ! Thou sun that burst out through the mist o'er the mountains, In that moment mine eyes met the field of his sorrow— Bear witness, ye fields that have fed me and clothed me, And air I have breathed, and earth that hast borne me— Though I find you but shadows, and wrought but for fading, Though all ye and God fail me,— my love shall not fail! Yea, even if this love, that seemeth such pleasure As earth is unworthy of, turneth to pain \

If he wake without memory of me and my weeping, With a name on his lips not mine— that I know not: If thus my hand leave his hand for the last time, And no word from his lips be kind for my comfort— If all speech fail between us, all sight fail me henceforth, If all hope and God fail me—my love shall not fail.

— Friend, I may not forbear : we have been here together: My hand on thy hand has been laid, and thou trembledst. Think now if this May sky should darken above us, And the death of the world in this minute should part us— Think, my love, of the loss if my lips had not kissed thee. And forgive me my hunger of no hope begotten! [She kisses him.

KING PHARAMOND (awaking).

Who art thou ? who art thou, that my dream I might tell thee ? How with words full of love she drew near me, and kissed me. O thou kissest me yet, and thou clingest about me ! Ah, kiss me and wake me into death and deliverance !

AZALAIS (drawing away from him).

Speak no rough word, I pray thee, for a little, thou loveliest! But forgive me, for the years of my life have been lonely, And thou art come hither with the eyes of one seeking.

KING PHARAMOND.

Sweet dream of old days, and her very lips speaking The words of my lips and the night season's longing. How might I have lived had I known what I longed for!

AZALAIS.

I knew thou wouldst love, I knew all thy desire— Am I she whom thou seekest ? may I draw nigh again ?

KING PHARAMOND.

Ah, lengthen no more the years of my seeking,
For thou knowest my love as thy love lies before me.

AZALAIS (coming near to him again).

0 Love, there was fear in thine eyes as thou wakenedst; Thy first words were of dreaming and death—but we die not.

KING PHARAMOND.

In thine eyes was a terror as thy lips' touches faded, Sore trembled thine arms as they fell away from me ; And thy voice was grown piteous with words of beseeching, So that still for a little my search seemed unended. —Ah, unending, unchanging desire fulfils me !

cry out for thy comfort as thou clingest about me.

O joy hard to bear, but for memory of sorrow, But for pity of past days whose bitter is sweet now ! Let us speak, love, together some word of our story, That our lips as they part may remember the glory.

AZALAIS.

O Love, kiss me into silence lest no word avail me; Stay my head with thy bosom lest breath and life fail me.

THE MUSIC.

LOVE is ENOUGH : while ye deemed him a-sleeping,

There were signs of his coming and sounds of his feet; His touch it was that would bring you to weeping,

When the summer was deepest and music most sweet:

In his footsteps ye followed the day to its dying, Ye went forth by his gown-skirts the morning to meet: In his place on the beaten-down orchard-grass lying, Of the sweet ways ye pondered yet left for life's trying.

Ah, what was all dreaming of pleasure anear you,

To the time when his eyes on your wistful eyes turned, And ye saw his lips move, and his head bend to hear you, As new-born and glad to his kindness ye yearned 1

Ah, what was all dreaming of anguish and sorrow, To the time when the world in his torment was burned. And no god your heart from its prison might borrow, And no rest was left, no today, no tomorrow ?

All wonder of pleasure, all doubt of desire, All blindness, are ended, and no more ye feel LOVE IS ENOUGH.

93

If your feet tread his flowers or the flames of his fire, If your breast meet his balms or the edge of his steel.

Change is come, and past over, no more strife, no more learning : Now your lips and your forehead are sealed with his seal,

Look backward and smile at the thorns and the burning.

— Sweet rest, O my soul, and no fear of returning!

Enter before the curtain LOVE, dad still as a Pilgrim.

LOVE.

HOW is it with the Fosterer then, when he Comes back again that rest and peace to see, And God his latest prayer has granted now?— Why, as the winds whereso they list shall blow, So drifts the thought of man, and who shall say Tomorrow shall my thought be as today ? —My fosterling is happy, and I too ; Yet did we leave behind things good to do, Deeds good to tell about when we are dead. Here is no pain, but rest, and easy bread; Yet therewith something hard to understand JDulls the crowned work to which I set my hand. Ah, patience yet! his longing is well won, And I shall die at last and all be done.— Such words unspoken the best man on earth Still bears about betwixt the lover's mirth; And now he hath what he went forth to find, This Pharamond is neither dull nor blind, And looking upon Oliver, he saith :— My friend recked nothing of his life or death, Knew not my anguish then, nor now my pleasure,

And by my crowned joy sets his lessened treasure.

Is risk of twenty days of wind and sea,

Of new-born feeble headless enmity,

I should have scorned once, too great gift to give

To this most faithful man that he may live ?

—Yea, was that all ? my faithful, you and I,

Still craving, scorn the world too utterly,

The world we want not—yet, our one desire

Fulfilled at last, what next shall feed the fire ?

— I say not this to make my altar cold;

Rather that ye, my happy ones, should hold

Enough of memory and enough of fear

Within your hearts to keep its flame full clear;
Rather that ye, still dearer to my heart,
Whom words call hapless, yet should praise your part,
Wherein the morning and the evening sun
Are bright about a story never done ;
That those for chastening, these for joy should cling
About the marvels that my minstrels sing.

Well, Pharamond fulfilled of love must turn Unto the folk that still he deemed would yearn To see his face, and hear his voice once more; And he was mindful of the days passed o'er,

And fain had linked them to these days of love; And he perchance was fain the world to move While love looked on , and he perchance was fain Some pleasure of the strife of old to gain. Easy withal it seemed to him to land, And by his empty throne awhile to stand Amid the wonder, and then sit him down While folk went forth to seek the hidden crown. Or else his name upon the same wind borne As smote the world with winding of his horn, His hood pulled back, his banner flung abroad, A gleam of sunshine on his half-drawn sword. —Well, he and you and I have little skill To know the secret of Fate's worldly will; Yet can I guess, and you belike may guess, Yea, and e'en he mid all his lordliness, That much may be forgot in three years' space Outside my kingdom.—Gone his godlike face, His calm voice, and his kindness, half akin Amid a blind folk to rebuke of sin, Men 'gin to think that he was great and good, But hindered them from doing as they would, And ere they have much time to think on it Between their teeth another has the bit, And forth they run with Force and Fate behind.

—Indeed his sword might somewhat heal the blind,
Were I not, and the softness I have given;
With me for him have hope and glory striven
In other days when my tale was beginning;
But sweet life lay beyond then for the winning,
And now what sweetness?—blood of men to spill
Who once believed him God to heal their ill:
To break the gate and storm adown the street
Where once his coming flower-crowned girls did greet:
To deem the cry come from amidst his folk
When his own country tongue should curse his stroke—
Nay, he shall leave to better men or worse
His people's conquered homage and their curse.

So forth they go, his Oliver and he, One thing at least to learn across the sea, That whatso needless shadows life may borrow Love is enough amidst of joy or sorrow.

Love is enough—My Faithful, in your eyes I see the thought, Our Lord is overwise Some minutes past in what concerns him not, And us no more : is all his tale forgot ? —Ah, Well-beloved, I fell asleep e'en now, And in my sleep some enemy did show

H

Sad ghosts of bitter things, and names unknown For things I know—a maze with shame bestrewn And ruin and death; till e'en myself did seem A wandering curse amidst a hopeless dream. —Yet see ! I live, no older than of old, What tales soe'er of changing Time has told. And ye who cling to all my hand shall give, Sorrow or joy, no less than I shall live.

Scene; Before KING PHARAMOND'S Palace.
KING PHARAMOND.

ALONG time it seems since this morn when I met them, The men of my household and the great man they honour Better counsel in king-choosing might I have given Had ye bided my coming back hither, my people : And yet who shall say or foretell what Fate meaneth ? For that man there, the stranger, Honorius men called him, I account him the soul to King Theobald's body, And the twain are one king ; and a goodly king may be For this people, who grasping at peace and good days, Careth little who giveth them that which they long for. Yet what gifts have I given them; I who this even Turn away with grim face from the fight that should try me ?

is just then, I have lost: lie down, thou supplanter, In thy tomb in the minster when thy life is well over, And the well-carven image of latten laid o'er thee Shall live on as thou livedst, and be worthy the praising Whereby folk shall remember the days of thy plenty. Praising Theobald the Good and the peace that he brought them, But I — I shall live too, though no graven image On the grass of the hill-side shall brave the storms' beating; Though through days of thy plenty the people remember

zoo LOVE IS ENOUGH.

As a dim time of war the past days of King Pharamond; Yet belike as time weareth, and folk turn back a little To the darkness where dreams lie and live on for ever, Even there shall be Pharamond who failed not in battle, But feared to overcome his folk who forgot him, And turned back and left them a tale for the telling, A song for the singing, that yet in some battle May grow to remembrance and rend through the ruin As my sword rent it through in the days gone for ever. So, like Enoch of old, I was not, for God took me. —But lo, here is Oliver, all draws to an ending —

Enter OLIVER.

Well met, my Oliver! the clocks strike the due minute. What news hast thou got?—thou art moody of visage.

MASTER OLIVER.

In one word, 'tis battle ; the days we begun with Must begin once again with the world waxen baser.

KING PHARAMOND.

Ah! battle it may be : but surely no river Runneth back to its springing : so the world has grown wiser And Theobald the Constable is king in our stead, Andcontenteth the folk who cried, ' Save us, King Pharamond !'

MASTER OLIVER.

Hast thou heard of his councillor men call Honorius ? Folk hold him in fear, and in love the tale hath it.

KING PHARAMOND.

Much of him have I heard : nay, more, I have seen him
With the men of my household, and the great man they honour.
They were faring afield to some hunt or disporting,
Few faces were missing, and many I saw there
I was fain of in days past at fray or at feasting;
My heart yearned towards them—but what—days have changed them,
They must wend as they must down the way they are driven.

MASTER OLIVER.

Yet e'en in these days there remaineth a remnant That is faithful and fears not the flap of thy banner.

KING PHARAMOND.

And a fair crown is faith, as thou knowest, my father; Fails the world, yet that faileth not; love hath begot it, Sweet life and contentment at last springeth from it; No helping these need whose hearts still are with me, Nay, rather they handle the gold rod of my kingdom.

to2 LOVE IS ENOUGH.

MASTER OLIVER.

Yet if thou leadest forth once more as aforetime In faith of great deeds will I follow thee, Pharamond, And thy latter end yet shall be counted more glorious Than thy glorious beginning; and great shall my gain be If e'en I must die ere the day of thy triumph.

KING PHARAMOND.

Dear is thy heart mid the best and the brightest, Yet not against these my famed blade will I bare.

MASTER OLIVER.

Nay, what hast thou heard of their babble and baseness ?

KING PHARAMOND.

Full enough, friend—content thee, my lips shall not speak it, The same hour wherein they have said that I love thee. Suffice it, folk need me no more: the deliverance, Dear bought in the days past, their hearts have forgotten, But faintly their dim eyes a feared face remember, -Their dull ears remember a stern voice they hated. What then, shall I waken their fear and their hatred, And then wait till fresh terror their memory awaketh, With the semblance of love that they have not to give me ?

Nay, nay, they are safe from my help and my justice, And I — I am freed, and fresh waxeth my manhood.

MASTER OLIVER.

It may not be otherwise since thou wilt have it,
Yet I say it again, if thou shake out thy banner,
Some brave men will be borne unto earth peradventure,
Many dastards go trembling to meet their due doom,
And then shall come fair days and glory upon me
And on all men on earth for thy fame, O King Pharamond.

KING PHARAMOND.

Yea, I was king once; the songs sung o'er my cradle
Were ballads prbattle_and deeds of my fathers:
Yea, Ijyas_King Pharamondj in no carpeted court-room
Bore they the corpse of my father before me ;
But on grass trodden grey by the hoofs of the war-steeds
Did I kneel to his white lips and sword-cloven bosom,
As from clutch of dead fingers his notched sword I caught;
For a furlong before us the spear-wood was glistening.
I was king of this city when here where we stand now
Amidst a grim silence I mustered all menfolk
Who might yet bear a weapon ; and no brawl of kings was it
That brought war on the city, and silenced the markets
And cumbered the haven with crowd of masts sailless,
But great countries arisen for our ruin and downfall.
I was king of the land, when on all roads were riding
The legates of proud princes to pray help and give service—

Yea, I was a great king at last as I sat there,
Peace spread far about me, and the love of all people
To my palace gates wafted by each wind of the heavens.
—And where sought I all this ? with what price did I buy it ?
Nay, for thou knowest that this fair fame and fortune
Came stealing soft-footed to give their gifts to me :
And shall I, who was king once, grow griping and weary
In unclosing the clenched fists of niggards who hold them,
These gifts that I had once, and, having, scarce heeded ?
Nay, one thing I have sought, I have sought and have found it,
And thou, friend, hast helped me and seest me made happy.
MASTER OLIVER.
Farewell then the last time, O land of my fathers!
Farewell, feeble hopes that I once held so mighty.
Yet no more have I need of but this word that thou sayest,
And nought have I to do but to serve thee, my master.
In what land of the world shall we dwell now henceforward ?
KING PHARAMOND.

In the land where my love our returning abideth, The poor land and kingless of the shepherding people, There is peace there, and all things this land are unlike to.
MASTER OLIVER.

Before the light waneth will I seek for a passage, Since for thee and for me the land groweth perilous: Yea, o'er sweet smell the flowers, too familiar the folk seem, Fain I grow of the salt seas, since all things are over here.
KING PHARAMOND.

I am fain of one hour's farewell in the twilight, To the times I lament not: times worser than these times, To the times that I blame not, that brought on times better— Let us meet in our hostel—be brave mid thy kindness, Let thy heart say, as mine saith, that fair life awaits us.
MASTER OLIVER.

Yea, no look in thy face is of ruin, O my master;
Thou art king yet, unchanged yet, nor is my heart changing;
The world hath no chances to conquer thy glory.
[Exit OLIVER.
KING PHARAMOND.

Full fair were the world if such faith were remembered. If such love as thy love had its due, O my fosterer. Forgive me that giftless from me thou departest, With thy gifts in my hands left. I might not but take them;

Thou wilt not begrudge me, I will not forget thee.— —Long fall the shadows and night draws on apace now, Day sighs as she sinketh back on to her pillow, And her last waking breath is full sweet with the rose. —In such wise depart thou, O daylight of life, Loved once for the shadows that told of the dreamtide ; Loved still for the longing whereby I remember That I was lone once in the world of thy making ; Lone wandering about on thy blind way's confusion, The maze of thy paths that yet led me to love. All is passed now, and passionless, faint are ye waxen, Ye hours of blind seeking full of pain clean forgotten, If it were not that e'en now her eyes I behold not, That the way lieth long to her feet that would find me, That the green seas delay yet her fair arms enfolding, That the long leagues of air will not bear the cry hither Wherewith she is crying, Come, love, for I love thee.

    _A trumpet sounds.

Hark ! O days grown a dream of the dream ye have won me, Do ye draw forth the ghosts of old deeds that were nothing, That the sound of my trumpet floats down on the even ? What shows will ye give me to grace my departure ? Hark !—the beat of the horse-hoofs, the murmur of men folk ! Am I riding from battle amidst of my faithful, Wild hopes in my heart of the days that are coming;

Wild longing unsatisfied clinging about me;
Full of faith that the summer sun elsewhere is ripening
The fruit grown a pain for my parched lips to think of?
—Come back, thou poor Pharamond ! come back for my pity !
Far afield must thou fare before the rest cometh;
In far lands are they raising the walls of thy prison,
Forging wiles for waylaying, and fair lies for lulling,
The faith and the fire of the heart the world hateth.
In thy way wax streams fordless, and choked passes pathless,
Fever lurks in the valley, and plague passeth over
The sand of the plain, and with venom and fury
Fulfilled are the woods that thou needs must wend through :
In the hollow of the mountains the wind is a-storing
Till the keel that shall carry thee hoisteth her sail;
War is crouching unseen round the lands thou shalt come to,
With thy sword cast away and thy cunning forgotten.
Yea, and e'en the great lord, the great Love of thy fealty,
He who goadeth thee on, weaveth nets to cast o'er thee.
—And thou knowest it all, as thou ridest there lonely,
With the tangles and toils of tomorrow's uprising
Making ready meanwhile for more days of thy kingship.
Faithful heart hadst thou, Pharamond, to hold fast thy treasure!
I am fain of thee : surely no shame hath destained thee;
Come hither, for thy face all unkissed would I look on!
—Stand we close, for here cometh King Theobald from the hunting.
Enter KING THEOBALD, HONORIUS^ and the people.
KING THEOBALD.
A fair day, my folk, have I had in your fellowship,
And as fair a day cometh tomorrow to greet us,
When the lord of the Golden Land bringeth us tribute :
Grace the gifts of my good-hap with your presence, I pray you.
THE PEOPLE.
God save Theobald the Good, the king of his people !
HONORIUS (aside).

Yea, save him! and send the Gold lords away satisfied, That the old sword of Pharamond, lying asleep there In the new golden scabbard, will yet bite as aforetime!

    [They pass away into the palace court.

KING PHARAMOND.

Troop past in the twilight, O pageant that served me, Pour through the dark archway to the light that awaits you In the chamber of dais where I once sat among you ! Like the shadows ye are to the shadowless glory Of the banquet-hall blazing with gold and light go ye : There blink for a little at your king in his bravery, Then bear forth your faith to the blackness of night-tide,

And fall asleep fearless of memories of Pharamond, And in dim dreams dream haply that ye too are kings —For your dull morrow cometh that is as today is.

Pass on in contentment, O king, I discerned not
Through the cloak of your blindness that saw nought beside thee,
That feared for no pain and craved for no pleasure !
Pass on, dead-alive, to thy place ! thou art worthy:
Nor shalt thou grow wearier than well-worshipped idol
That the incense winds round in the land of the heathen,
While the early and latter rains fall as God listeth,
And on earth that God loveth the sun riseth daily.
—Well art thou : for wert thou the crown of all rulers,
No field shouldst thou ripen, free no frost-bounden river,
Loose no heart from its love, turn no soul to salvation,
Thrust no tempest aside, stay no plague in mid ocean,
Yet grow unto thinking that thou wert God's brother,
Till loveless death gripped thee unloved, unlamented.
— Pass forth, weary King, bear thy crown high tonight!
Then fall asleep, fearing no cry from times bygone,
But in dim dreams dream haply that thou art desired,
—For thy dull morrow cometh, and is as today is.

Ah, hold ! now there flashes a link in the archway, And its light falleth full on thy face, O Honorius,

no LOVE IS ENOUGH.

And I know thee the land's lord, and far away fadeth My old life of a king at the sight, O thou stranger ! For I know thee full surely the foe the heart hateth For that barren fulfilment of all that it lacketh. I may turn away praising that those days long departed Departed without thee— how long had I piped then Or e'er thou hadst danced, how long were my weeping Ere thou hadst lamented ! — What dear thing desired Would thy heart e'er have come to know why I craved for! To what crime I could think of couldst thou be consenting ? Yet thou — well I know thee most meet for a ruler— -Thou lovest not mercy, yet shalt thou be merciful; Thou joy'st not in justice, yet just shall thy dooms be; No deep hell thou dreadest, nor dream'st of high heaven ; No gleam of love leads thee; no gift men may give thee; For no kiss, for no comfort the lone way thou wearest, A blind will without life, lest thou faint ere the end come. — Yea, folly it was when I called thee my foeman ; From thee may I turn now with sword in the scabbard Without shame or misgiving, because God hath made thee A ruler for manfolk : pass on then unpitied ! There is darkness between us till the measure's fulfilment. Amidst singing thou hear'st not, fair sights that thou seest not, Think this eve on the deeds thou shalt set in men's hands To bring fair days about for which thou hast no blessing.

Then fall asleep fearless of dead days that return not; Yet dream if thou may'st that thou yet hast a hope ! —For thy dull morrow cometh and is as today is.

O sweet wind of the night, wherewith now ariseth
The red moon through the garden boughs frail, overladen,
O faint murmuring tongue of the dream-tide triumphant,

That wouldst tell me sad tales in the times long passed over,
If somewhat I sicken and turn to your freshness,
From no shame it is of earth's tangle and trouble,
And deeds done for nought, and change that forgetteth ;
But for hope of the lips that I kissed on the sea-strand,
But for hope of the hands that clung trembling about me,—
And the breast that was heaving with words driven backward,
By longing I longed for, by pain of departing,
By my eyes that knew her pain, my pain that might speak not—
Yea, for hope of the morn when the sea is passed over,
And for hope of the next moon the elm-boughs shall tangle j
And fresh dawn, and fresh noon, and fresh night of desire
Still following and changing, with nothing forgotten;
For hope of new wonder each morn, when I, waking
Behold her awaking eyes turning to seek me ;
For hope of fresh marvels each time the world changing
Shall show her feet moving in noontide to meet me;
For hope of fresh bliss, past all words, half forgotten,
When her voice shall break through the hushed blackness of night.
— O sweet wind of the summer-tide, broad moon a-whitening,
Bear me witness to Love, and the world he has fashioned !
It shall change, we shall change, as through rain and through sunshine
The green rod of the rose-bough to blossoming changeth :
Still lieth in wait with his sweet tale untold of
Each long year of Love, and the first scarce beginneth,
Wherein I have hearkened to the word God hath whispered,
Why the fair world was fashioned mid wonders uncounted.
Breathe soft, O sweet wind, for surely she speaketh :
Weary I wax, and my life is a-waning;
Life, lapsethfast, and I faint for thee, Pharamond,
What are thou lacking if Love no more sufficeth ? —Weary not, sweet, as I weary to meet thee ; Look not on the long way but my eyes that were weeping Faint not in love as thy Pharamond fainteth !— —Yea, Love were enough if thy lips were not lacking.
THE MUSIC.
LOVE is ENOUGH : ho ye who seek saving,
Go no further; come hither; there have been who have found it, And these know the House of Fulfilment of Craving;
These know the Cup with the roses around it;
These know the World's Wound and the balm that hath bound it: Cry out, the World heedeth not, ' Love, lead us home f
He leadeth, He hearkeneth, He cometh to you-ward;
Set your faces as steel to the fears that assemble Round his goad for the faint, and his scourge for thefroward:
Lo his lips, how with tales of last kisses they tremble !
Lo his eyes of all sorrow that may not dissemble ! Cry out, for he heedeth, i O Love, lead us home /'

O hearken the words of his voice of compassion: ' Come cling round about me, ye faithful who sicken

Of the weary unrest and the world's passing fashion ! As the rain in mid-morning your troubles shall thicken, But surely within you some Godhead doth quicken,

As ye cry to me heeding, and leading you home.

(Come — pain ye shall have, and be blind to the ending ! Come — fear ye shall have, mid the sky's overcasting !

Come — change ye shall have, for far are ye wending!

Come — no crown ye shall have for your thirst and your fasting, But the kissed lips of Love and fair life everlasting !

Cry out, for one heedeth, who leadeth you home /'

Is he gone ? was he with us ? — ho ye who seek saving, Go no further; come hither; for have we not found it ?

Here is the House of Fulfilment of Craving ; Here is the Cup with the roses around it; The World's Wound well healed, and the balm that hath bound it.

Cry out! for he heedeth, fair Love that led home.

Enter before the curtain, LOVE, holding a crown and palm-branch.

LOVE.

IF love be real, if I whom ye behold Be aught but glittering wings and gown of gold, Be aught but singing of an ancient song Made sweet by record of dead stingless wrong, How shall we part at that sad garden's end Through which the ghosts of mighty lovers wend? How shall ye faint and fade with giftless hands Who once held fast the' life of all the lands ? — Beloved, if so much as this I say, I know full well ye need it not to-day, As with full hearts and glorious hope ablaze Through the thick veil of what shall be ye gaze, And lacking words to name the things ye see Turn back with yearning speechless mouths to me.— —Ah, not today — and yet the time has been When by the bed my wings have waved unseen Wherein my servant lay who deemed me dead ; My tears have dropped anigh the hapless head Deep buried in the grass and crying out For heaven to fall, and end despair or doubt: Lo, for such days I speak and say, believe That from these hands reward ye shall receive.

— Reward of what ?—Life springing fresh again.— Life of delight?—I say it not—Of pain?

It may be—Pain eternal?—Who may tell? Yet pain of Heaven, beloved, and not of Hell. —What sign, what sign, ye cry, that so it is? -^The sign of Earth, its sorrow and its bliss, Waxing and waning, steadfastness and change; Too full of life that I should think it strange Though death hang over it; too sure to die But I must deem its resurrection nigh.

— In what wise, ah, in what wise shall it be ? How shall the bark that girds the winter tree Babble about the sap that sleeps beneath, And tell the fashion of its life and death?

How shall my tongue in speech man's longing wrought Tell of the things whereof he knoweth nought ? Should I essay it might ye understand How those I love shall share my promised land ! x-Then must I speak of little things as great, Then must I tell of love and call it hate, Then must I bid you seek what all men shun, Reward defeat, praise deeds that were not done.

Have faith, and crave and suffer, and all ye The many mansions of my house shall see

In all content: cast shame and pride away, Let honour gild the world's eventless day, Shrink not from change, and shudder not at crime, Leave lies to rattle in the sieve of Time ! Then, whatsoe'er your workday gear shall stain, Of me a wedding-garment shall ye gain No God shall dare cry out at, when at last Your time of ignorance is overpast j A wedding garment, and a glorious seat Within my household, e'en as yet be meet.

Fear not, I say again ; believe it true That not as men mete shall I measure you : This calm strong soul, whose hidden tale found out Has grown a spell to conquer fear and doubt, Is he not mine ? yea, surely—mine no less This well mocked clamourer out of bitterness : The strong one's strength, from me he had it not; Let the world keep it that his love forgot The weak one's weakness was enough to save, Let the world hide it in his honour's grave ! For whatso folly is, or wisdom was Across my threshold naked all must pass.

Fear not; no vessel to dishonour born
Is in my house ; there all shall well adorn
The walls whose stones the lapse of Time has laid.
Behold again; this life great stories ma
All cast aside for love, and then and then
Love niched away; the world an adder-den,
And all folk foes; and one, the one desire—
— How shall we name it?—grown a poisoned fire,' God once, God still, but God of wrong and shame A lying God, a curse without a name.

So turneth love to hate, the wise world saith.
— Folly—I say 'twixt love and hate lies death, They shall not mingle : neither died this love,

But through a dreadful world all changed must move With earthly death and wrong, and earthly woe The only deeds its hand might find to do. Surely ye deem that this one shall abide Within the murmuring palace of my pride.

But lo another, how shall he have praise ? Through flame and thorns I led him many days And nought he shrank, but smiled and followed close, Till in his path the shade of hate arose 'Twixt him and his desire : with heart that burned For very love back through the thorns he turned, His wounds, nis tears, his prayers without avail

Forgotten now, nor e'en for him a tale ; Because for love's sake love he cast aside.
— Lo, saith the World, a heart well satisfied With what I give, a barren love forgot—
— Draw near me, O my child, and heed them not! The world thou lovest, e'en my world it is,

Thy faithful hands yet reach out for my bliss, Thou seest me in the night and in the day Thou canst not deem that I can go astray.

No further, saith the world 'twixt Heaven and Hell
Than 'twixt these twain.—My faithful, heed it well!
For on the great day when the hosts are met
On Armageddon's plain by spears beset,
This is my banner with my sign thereon,
That is my sword wherewith my deeds are done.

But how shall tongue of man tell all the tale Of faithful hearts who overcome or fail, But at the last fail nowise to be mine. In diverse ways they drink the fateful wine Those twain drank mid the lulling of the storm Upon the Irish Sea, when love grown warm Kindled and blazed, and lit the days to come, The hope and joy and death that led them home.

—In diverse ways; yet having drunk, be sure
The flame thus lighted ever shall endure,
So my feet trod the grapes whereby it glowed.

Lo. Faithful, lo, the door of my abode
Wide open now, and many pressing in
That they the lordship of the World may win!
Hark to the murmuring round my bannered car,
And gird your weapons to you for the war!
For who shall say how soon the day shall be
Of that last fight that swalloweth up the sea ?
Fear not, be ready! forth the banners go,
And will not turn again till every foe
Is overcome as though they had not been.
Then, with your memories ever fresh and green,
Come back within the House of Love to dwell;
For ye—the sorrow that no words might tell,
Your tears unheeded, and your prayers made nought
Thus and no otherwise through all have wrought,
That if, the while ye toiled and sorrowed most
The sound of your lamenting seemed all lost,
And from my land no answer came again,
It was because of that your care and pain
A house was building, and your bitter sighs
Canie hither as toil-helping melodies,

And in the mortar of our gem-built wall Your tears were mingled mid the rise and fall Of golden trowels tinkling in the hands Of builders gathered wide from all the lands.— — Is the house finished? Nay, come help to build Walls that the sun of sorrow once did gild Through many a bitter morn and hopeless eve, That so at last in bliss ye may believe; Then rest with me, and turn no more to tears, For then no more by days and months and years, By hours of pain come back, and joy passed o'er We measure time that was—and is no more.

JOAN.

THE afternoon is waxen grey

Now these fair shapes have passed away And I, who should be merry now A-thinking of the glorious show, Feel somewhat sad, and wish it were Tomorrow's mid-morn fresh and fair

About the babble of our stead.

GILES.

Content thee, sweet, for nowise dead Within our hearts the story is It shall come back to better bliss On many an eve of happy spring, Or midst of summer's flourishing. Or think—some noon of autumn-tide Thou wandering on the turf beside The chestnut-wood may'st find thy song Fade out, as slow thou goest along, Until at last thy feet stay there As though thou bidedst something fair, And hearkenedst for a coming foot; While down the bole unto the root

The long leaves flutter loud to thee The fall of spiky nuts shall be, And creeping wood-wale's noise above; For thou wouldst see the wings of Love.

JOAN.

Or some November eve belike
Thou wandering back with bow and tyke
From wolf-chase on the wind-swept hill
Shall find that narrow vale and still,
And Pharamond and Azalais

Amidmost of that grassy place
Where we twain met last year, whereby
Red-shafted pine-trunks rise on high,
And changeless now from year to year,
What change soever brought them there,
Great rocks are scattered all around :
—Wouldst thou be frightened at the sound
Of their soft speech ? So long ago
It was since first their love did grow.
GILES.
Maybe: for e'en now when he turned, His heart's scorn and his hate outburned,
And love the more for that ablaze, I shuddered, e'en as in the place High up the
mountains, where men say Gods dwelt in time long worn away.
JOAN.
At Love's voice did I tremble too, And his bright wings, for all I knew He was a comely
minstrel-lad, In dainty golden raiment clad.
GILES.
Yea, yea; for though today he spake Words measured for our pleasure's sake, From well-
taught mouth not overwise, Yet did that fount of speech arise In days that ancient folk called old.
O long ago the tale was told To mighty men of thought and deed, Who kindled hearkening their
own need, Set forth by long-forgotten men, E'en as we kindle : praise we then Tales of old time,
whereby alone The fairness of the world is shown.
JOAN.
A longing yet about me clings, As I had hearkened half-told things j And better than the
words make plain I seem to know these lovers twain. Let us go hence, lest there should fall
Something that yet should mar it all.
GILES.
Hist—Master Mayor is drawn anigh ; The Empress speaketh presently.
THE MAYOR.
May it please you, your Graces, that I be forgiven, Over-bold, over-eager to bear forth
my speech, In which yet there speaketh the Good Town, beseeching That ye tell us of your
kindness if ye be contented With this breath of old tales, and shadowy seemings Of old times
departed.—Overwise for our pleasure May the rhyme be perchance; but rightly we knew not
How to change it and fashion it fresh into fairness. And once more, your Graces, we pray your
forgiveness For the boldness Love gave us to set forth this story ; And again, that I say, all that
Pharamond sought for, Through sick dreams and weariness, now have ye found,
Mid health and in wealth, and in might to uphold us;
Midst our love who shall deem you our hope and our treasure.
Well all is done now; so forget ye King Pharamond,
And Azalais his love, if we set it forth foully,
That fairly set forth were a sweet thing to think of
In the season of summer betwixt labour and sleeping.
THE EMPEROR.
Fair Master Mayor, and City well beloved,
Think of us twain as folk no little moved
By this your kindness ; and believe it not

That Pharamond the Freed shall be forgot,
By us at least: yea, more than ye may think,
This summer dream into our hearts shall sink.
Lo, Pharamond longed and toiled, nor toiled in vain ;
But fame he won : he longed and toiled again,
And Love he won : 'twas a long time ago,
And men did swiftly what we now do slow,
And he, a great man full of gifts and grace,
Wrought out a twofold life in ten years' space.
Ah, fair sir, if for me reward come first,
Yet will I hope that ye have seen the worst
Of that my kingcraft, that I yet shall earn
Some part of that which is so long to learn.
Now of your gentleness I pray you bring
This knife and girdle, deemed a well-wrought thing; And a king's thanks, whatso they be of worth, To him who Pharamond this day set forth In worthiest wise, and made a great man live, Giving me greater gifts than I may give.

THE EMPRESS.
And therewithal I pray you, Master Mayor,
Unto the seeming Azalais to bear
This chain, that she may wear it for my sake,
The memory of my pleasure to awake. [Exit MA VOR.

THE EMPEROR.
Gifts such as kings give, sweet! Fain had I been To see him face to face and his fair Queen, And thank him friendly; asking him maybe How the world looks to one with love left free : It may not be, for as thine eyes say, sweet, Few folk as friends shall unfreed Pharamond meet. So is it: we are lonelier than those twain, Though from their vale they ne'er depart again.

THE EMPRESS.
Shall I lament it, love, since thou and I
By all the seeming pride are drawn more nigh ?
Lo, love, our toil-girthed garden of desire, How of its changeless sweetness may we tire, While round about the storm is in the boughs And careless change amid the turmoil ploughs The rugged fields we needs must stumble o'er, Till the grain ripens that shall change no more.

THE EMPEROR.
Yea, and an omen fair we well may deem This dreamy shadowing of ancient dream, Of what our own hearts long for on the day When the first furrow cleaves the fallow grey.

THE" EMPRESS.
O fair it is ! let us go forth, my sweet, And be alone amid the babbling street; Yea, so alone that scarce the hush of night May add one joy unto our proved delight.

GILES.
Fair lovers were they: I am fain To see them both ere long again; Yea, nigher too, if it might be.

JOAN.
Too wide and dim, love, lies the sea, That we should look on face to face This Pharamond and Azalais. Those only from the dead come back Who left behind them what they lack.

GILES.

Nay, I was asking nought so strange, Since long ago their life did change : The seeming King and Queen I meant. And e'en now 'twas my full intent To bid them home to us straightway, And crown the joyance of to-day. He may be glad to see my face, He first saw mid that waggon race When the last barley-sheaf came home.

JOAN.

A great joy were it, should they come. They are dear lovers, sure enough. He deems the summer air too rough To touch her" kissed cheek, howsoe'er Through winter mountains they must fare, He would bid spring new flowers to make

K

Before her feet, that oft must ache With flinty driftings of the waste. And sure is she no more abased Before the face of king and lord, Than if the very Pharamond's sword Her love amid the hosts did wield Above the dinted lilied shield: O bid them home with us, and we Their scholars for a while will be In many a lesson of sweet lore To learn love's meaning more and more.

GILES.

And yet this night of all the year
Happier alone perchance they were,
And better so belike would seem
The glorious lovers of the dream :
So let them dream on lip to lip :
Yet will I gain his fellowship
Ere many days be o'er my head,
And they shall rest them in our stead;
And there we four awhile shall dwell
As though the world were nought but well,
And that old time come back again
When nought in all the earth had pain.

The sun through lime-boughs where we dine Upon my father's cup shall shine; The vintage of the river-bank, That ten years since the sunbeams drank, Shall fill the mazer bowl carved o'er With naked shepherd-folk of yore. Dainty should seem worse fare than ours As o'er the close-thronged garden flowers The wind comes to us, and the bees Complain overhead mid honey-trees.

JOAN. Wherewith shall we be garlanded?

GILES. For thee the buds of roses red.

JOAN. For her white roses widest blown.

GILES. The jasmine boughs for Pharamond's crown.

JOAN. And sops-in-vine for thee, fair love.

GILES.

Surely our feast shall deeper move The kind heart of the summer-tide Than many a day of pomp and pride ; And as by moon and stars well lit Our kissing lips shall finish it, Full satisfied our hearts shall be With that well-won felicity.

JOAN.

Ah, sweetheart, be not all so sure: Love, who beyond all worlds shall dure, Mid pleading sweetness still doth keep A goad to stay his own from sleep ; And I shall long as thou shalt long

For unknown cure of unnamed wrong As from our happy feast we pass Along the rose-strewn midnight grass — — Praise Love who will not be forgot!

GILES.

Yea, praise we Love who sleepeth not!

—Come, o'er much gold mine eyes have seen,

And long now for the pathway green,

And rose-hung ancient walls of grey Yet warm with sunshine gone away.

JOAN.

Yea, full fain would I rest thereby, And watch the flickering martins fly About the long eave-bottles red And the clouds lessening overhead : E'en now meseems the cows are come Unto the grey gates of our home, And low to hear the milking-pail: The peacock spreads abroad his tail Against the sun, as down the lane The milkmaids pass the moveless wain, And stable door, where the roan team An hour agone began to dream Over the dusty oats.—

Come, love,

Noises of river and of grove And moving things in field and stall And night-birds' whistle shall be all Of the world's speech that we shall hear By then we come the garth anear : For then the moon that hangs aloft These thronged streets, lightless now and soft

Unnoted, yea, e'en like a shred Of yon wide white cloud overhead, Sharp in the dark star-sprinkled sky Low o'er the willow boughs shall lie ; And when our chamber we shall gain Eastward our drowsy eyes shall strain If yet perchance the dawn may show. — O Love, go with us as we go, And from the might of thy fair hand Cast wide about the blooming land The seed of such-like tales as this ! —O Day, change round about our bliss, Come, restful night, when day is done ! Come, dawn, and bring a fairer one !

THE END.

Made in the USA
Coppell, TX
06 April 2025

47976222R00031